THE MAN WHO D

<u>*THE MAN WH*</u>

<u>EARTH</u>

THE MAN WHO DIDN'T WANT TO GO TO EARTH

COPYRIGHT
The Man Who Didn't Want To Go To Earth by Michael Lighten. All Rights Reserved.

THE MAN WHO DIDN'T WANT TO GO TO EARTH

DEDICATIONS
For all those who woke up on Earth and found it overwhelming.

THE MAN WHO DIDN'T WANT TO GO TO EARTH

AUTHOR'S NOTES

Of course, these are fictional accounts of futuristic events. Each timeline is distinct by their standings.

I would encourage a gleaming of the forward glossary for Other Worldly Alien (OWA) expressions and brief history before devouring the whole text and story.

In addition, this is a story written off-world and had little effect on Earth's timeline, but Planet Phaes is the twin of Earth and whatever happens to Phaes (brother), can affect in a positive or negative fashion, Earth (sister).

I also adjusted the human=Human, fuman=Fuman, bolaris=Bolaris, phasee=Phasee, for a sign of respect to all the races in my book. Hope this clarifies some things.

THE MAN WHO DIDN'T WANT TO GO TO EARTH

EXTENDED GLOSSARY

Phasee's physical traits: Enlarged head with strong neck muscles. Most were tall in stature, at least six to seven feet with a Humanoid build with gray or white pupils.

With white pupils they still had excellent eyesight and superb memories. They also had two hearts, one smaller than the other. This attributed to the heavy gravity on planet Phaes.

The Phasees on Phaes have been known to live up to 600 years. On Earth, the average Phasee could live up to 100 years or more; but statistics were not yet in.

When rough man Mars returned to Phaes he ascertained the Phasees could become extinct within 100 years due to their two hearts, one heart not needed to compensate for the heavy gravity that was on Phaes.

He knew in time the smaller heart would slow its beat and stop beating altogether, which could cause the smaller heart to be removed to save the patient.

Fuman's physical traits: Fuman, a blend of Human and Phasee genes. Fumans averaged five to six feet in height and did resemble Phasee features, but with smaller heads and neck muscles.

Fumans were known to have two hearts, many of them were born with a smaller heart, which was usually surgically removed between the ages of 10 and 12, when the child was strong enough for the procedure.

Fuman's immune systems were unstable due to the combination of Phasee and Human

THE MAN WHO DIDN'T WANT TO GO TO EARTH

genes and had been known to die suddenly from body illnesses like colds and the flu. Fumans were known to be more empathic than Phasees who were more analytical and thus stronger mentally than Fumans.

Bolaris' physical traits: The Bolaris (or bos for Short) were hairy and resembled an appeasing, intelligent gorilla with some body hairs. Many bos were tall, six to seven feet and had small faces, beady eyes, and a muscular build. Their teeth resembled canine and their fingernails/toenails curved like claws if left uncut.

Through the amalgamation of various Humanoid species on Earth the Bolaris' began to lose their canine features and their love of meat. Many bos began to eat greens in their diet and some nibbled-on fruit.

Harmonic Aliens' physical traits: Better known as "HAS." They were tall aliens mixed with Other Worldly Alien (OWA) blood that transformed Humans, Fuman, Phasee, and Bolaris into their image. Harmonic Aliens were usually tall (near eight feet) and had vacant doll eyes that looked lifeless.

The HAS confirmed their vibrations kept away a species known as the Destroyers (or spider-crabs) a creature that devoured individuals; so many, in fear of the spider-crabs, volunteered to be merged to help in the harmonics.

In time the HAS had merged their DNA into various Humanoid species on Earth and by 2160 there were a recorded 394 on Earth.

THE MAN WHO DIDN'T WANT TO GO TO EARTH

PHAES: A planet over 300 light years from Earth. Phaes continued through warfare and eventually found peace. Over 7 million of their species left the war-torn planet and came to Earth, but Earth's gravitational pull and cataclysmic event destroyed 5 of their ships. Earthlings unfortunately saw their landing as a prelude to war and this caused the first Phasee/Human war.

PHASEES: An alien species from Phaes.

CATACLYSMIC EVENTS 2024: The shifting of the Earth's axis due to pollution that seeped into the grounds, waters, etc. The cataclysm wiped out 2/3 of the Earth's population through Earthquakes and tidal waves. After nearly 100 years of the event, the cataclysm could be traced between 2020 and 2025, respectively.

THE VANISHERS: Flesh eating creatures from a distant star that came to Earth in the nineteen-sixties to act as scientists. When one of their experiments killed a couple, they fled Earth but returned later to stay and amalgamate with Humans. The genetic combination of Human and vanisher were named Bolaris from Bolera a town in the Ozark region, but this term was soon lost, and Bolivar became the source of Bolaris/Human gene connections.

7

THE MAN WHO DIDN'T WANT TO GO TO EARTH

FUMANS: Mixture of Phasee and Human genes. Fumans who had babies called them fus (pronounced "foo's").

ROUGH MEN: Thirty *Fumans* placed in positions of power as future leaders worldwide. They were called rough men because of the harsh conditions they had to endure and remain focused on their purpose to keep the regions stabilized. Gradually many rough men died or were replaced by others.

THE ANCIENTS: Two Phasees who were sent from Phaes as a compassionate mission to help the Phasees on Earth survive under harsh conditions. In time Phasees were abandoned when the ancients in conflict with Vanishers introduced "Fumans" as a new species. This started the bofu wars.

HAS: (Harmonic Aliens) through merging with each species on Earth the *HAS* wanted a more harmonious Earth with sound and light that was positive and in unity with the Universal Force. The Harmonic Aliens could see in the future and acted as scribes and teachers of world leaders.

Juice Children or JC: Juice children were individuals with enhanced abilities through cell manipulation by the rough men.
Four women were picked by the rough men to carry to term. Some children or fus were born with no vocal cords, and some had expanded physical and mental capabilities.

THE MAN WHO DIDN'T WANT TO GO TO EARTH

BLANK PAGE MOVEMENT: A movement developed from 2055-2085 to train its members how to block their thoughts and emotions from others. *Blank Pagers,* as they were called, had an estimated 8 million members worldwide. This number was a low estimate, and 10-11 million members were guesstimated.

The Blank Page Movement (BPM) was used as a counter to Phasee and Fuman ways of reading emotions and thoughts, which left privacy laws in shambles, and not able to adapt to the unfamiliar environment of mental and emotional probes.

PLANET EXCURSIONS: When citizens from various planets agreed to visit other worlds for a fee. Planet Excursions were expensive, but some citizens went free for their service to the government of that world.

FUMAN-PHASEE EARTH CONNECTION: Or **FPEC** was a program developed on Phaes in 2027 (Earth years) with genetic connections. Human blood was drawn on Earth and merged with Phasee blood to develop Fuman soldiers.

When the Harmonic Aliens redesigned the Phasee to become calmer and less violent the Fumans on Phaes acted as cannon-fodder to ensure continuation of the Phasee species in case of war.

In time Phasees feared the Fumans and rough men from Earth, because of their aggressive tendencies and wanted to isolate them on an island where they could be easily watched, but this never

THE MAN WHO DIDN'T WANT TO GO TO EARTH

transpired due to Phaes' continued climatic problems.

THE 6 NEW SPECIES OF MAN ON EARTH: (1) Phasees, **(2)** Fumans, **(3)** Bolaris or Bos, **(4)** Bofus or Fubos, **(5)** Harmonic Aliens, **(6)** Jaycees (Juice Children).

THE DESTROYERS: a species that had technological expertise and resembled large black spider-crabs able to jump many feet to consume. Many planets fell because of their voracious appetite for blood and flesh. What kept the spider-crabs at bay were the Harmonic Aliens, able to absorb the spider-crabs.

HAS made a pact with the spider-crabs who had to do their bidding or be absorbed; but even HAS had *known* it would be a matter of time before the spider-crabs found a way around their Harmonics.

This day was dreaded and inevitable. So, in 2176 the spider-crabs made a move on Earth, Phaes and various planets; but were defeated at great cost...

THE MAN WHO DIDN'T WANT TO GO TO EARTH

<u>SERVANT ROBOTS' MODELS 2177</u>
Tall Robots A Version
TR B Version or Ba robots
TR C Version or Ca robots
TR D Version or Da robots
TR E Version or Ea. Robots

THE MAN WHO DIDN'T WANT TO GO TO EARTH

PROLOGUE

After the initial devastation of Phaes through underground Earth tremors and unstable, buried rockets, Earth was left without a planetary protector, and this unnerved many inhabitants.

The Harmonic Aliens developed a wormhole to assist in planet travel between the species, but this also was a prelude to new challenges.

With Earth open to planetary inhabitants that came through the wormhole, Earth became a hotbed of clashing cultures, laws, and remained in flux when it came to a variety of ideas.

Many saw war between the planets as imminent.

Enter the great distributor a foreigner from another planet who did not really want to go to Earth.

But he went anyway…

THE MAN WHO DIDN'T WANT TO GO TO EARTH

MAHATMA GHANDI QUOTE
"Earth provides enough to satisfy every man's needs, but not every man's greed."

THE MAN WHO DIDN'T WANT TO GO TO EARTH

1

(Written on Planet Urb)

On Planet Urb we were called Urbanites and on Planet Jan the natives were called Janeites. Planet Phaes, which was destroyed after the destroyer war were filled with Phasees. Then, there was Planet Pro, and I believe we sometimes referred to them as Proletarians.

We sometimes did not use that, but asked them if they were from Pro or if they were travelling to Pro.

On Earth, for which this book was written, our Proletarian was different than your form on Earth which dealt in economics. Ours was an entire species.

Also, I wrote this through *your* form of communication.

Our form of communication is thought with various sounds of approval or disapproval expressed through the lips and facial expressions, connected to thought transfer.

Our vocal language was long dead, sometimes used in robots through audio when there was a defect in their information circuit to process thoughts.

So, I wrote all this in a dead language then modified it to the Earth form of communication as close to the truth as possible. I hope I did a great job.

You don't know me from your first man, Adam (or your version of the Adam story). I am from Planet Urb, and I am a writer of reports to

THE MAN WHO DIDN'T WANT TO GO TO EARTH

present to a body of ten individuals on Urb, called the Elders Council.

The Elders Council were ancient, many of them over five-hundred long years (four-hundred and ninety of your Earth Years) and produced or rescinded laws on Urb.

We had a Great Leader Can, two-hundred and ninety-eight long years, who acted as an Authoritarian, where everything he wished and said happened, if he stayed within the laws of Urb.

Of course, these laws were used on a gray-area basis, when needed; if not, there was a fine line Can and his constituents could walk without getting in trouble from the Elders Council.

Trouble was in the form of prison for ten long years, a usual sentence for thievery, or death for much serious offenses like killing or rape.

I am only two-hundred and one year's long, but there were times I wanted to kill someone, but didn't have the heart to do it.

I knew if I commenced with that thought into action, I would have been surely caught with thought projection, internal microphones, and video spots. So far, we do not know on my planet who got away with what, but we believe over 90 % were caught through our means.

Any misunderstandings or bad blood usually simmered and ebbed away as I grew older. I tried not to hold grudges. I found them to be disabling for future ventures. Never knew when you would run into those same individuals along the way.

As it came to rape and murder on our planet, we had harsh laws.

THE MAN WHO DIDN'T WANT TO GO TO EARTH

If a child on our planet was raped there was instant death, because that was totally unacceptable by the Elders.

A full-grown individual was considered fifteen long turns and could be debated in the courts as miscommunication or mixed signals between them when it came to sexual overtures.

It always eluded me how someone could rape another full-grown individual, when it was freely given on our planet as through companionship (our form of a marriage where you could have as many companions as you and your partner was committed too) and a night person (an individual you slept with for one or two short nights for pleasure and comfort).

With something so free to give the Elders felt the individual had to be corrupt to the core to force sex, which was about domination.

Our form of forced death was totally different than your Earth forms of forced death. We locked their hands before them and placed a contraption on their head and fried the brain until their life signs dissipated. It was quick, but a brutal way of death.

Before you judge us, it was like your electric chair to put prisoners to death, but in a more concise form.

Our history was not like your history as you suspect. We all originated in Jan and traveled to other planets after thousands of years of technological expertise that improved our lives.

The other planets like Pro, Urb and Phaes had to be altered as it came to climate to fit our needs. We included injections to take away many

THE MAN WHO DIDN'T WANT TO GO TO EARTH

of the side effects, but the injections had side effects and it turned some dark (Urb) and some a mixture of light and dark (Phaes).

Janeites had almost a red skin tone and was the original skin tone of all of us, before other planetary incursions, injections and climate effects.

In Pro their complexion was a high pink, and they were tall, compared to Humans, averaging from six to seven feet tall.

Without the machines on Urb, Pro and Phaes we would be subject to its harsh conditions, and it could shorten our long life almost down to two-hundred long turns or less (190) of your Earth years.

In the beginning we moved from Jan to Pro, then to Urb. The last planet we terraformed was Phaes, where the Phasees began to branch out and move to Earth, while you went through cataclysmic planet destruction.

Our idea for God was used in intense prayer when we began to fight planet against planet in a barter and trade war that truly got out of hand so that billions died.

Our God was a search within to the still small voice from master-teachers' eons ago who taught millions the way to God.

Many of our councils on each planet guided the inhabitants to seek the God within to find great error in these wars that almost lasted a century.

We had no churches, mosques, or synagogues to go to, but searched within to find the answer and decided to end these wars, which was one raid after the other, ship to ship, bomb to bomb,

THE MAN WHO DIDN'T WANT TO GO TO EARTH

in our time of 2,000,385, like your Earth years, where we had records eons ago of the start of our species from Jan.

The Harmonic Aliens arrived nearly two-hundred long turns ago and helped to end our wars of domination and introduced us to the destroyers, a large jumping spider able to consume flesh.

This was before we realized they were not organic and a robotic form of an invention that got out of control, its inventor long dead from his own creation.

The going theory is that the Harmonic Aliens used the destroyers to force compliance on certain worlds; you either complied through Harmonic absorption or be consumed by the spider-crabs. The choice was obvious, especially if you had arachnophobia.

In this sense I agreed with the Harmonic Aliens, if you did not comply through compassion, which their vibrations represented you were for war and got what you deserved.

Sounds harsh, but there it was. Through the Harmonic Aliens or the blues on Earth they turned around our ways of war and we saw another side of life. A better side but not always a brighter side.

This segued me to the events on Earth, which I had no desire to learn about. I wrote this after the events catapulted me to that place. I was not a party to this event at all.

My tenure as a *Great Distributor* (their words not mine) led me before the Elders Council on your Earth year of 2186.

THE MAN WHO DIDN'T WANT TO GO TO EARTH

I arrived at the Elder's Council of Urb in your Earth year of 2186.

As the massive gray doors parted I stood for a moment, unsure to enter, but the image of my mother caused a smile to go across my face; so, I entered a little more comfortably.

My mother was on the Elders Council. She was the youngest at five-hundred and eighty-two long turns (582). Her eyes glistened on seeing me, for we had not seen each other for four long turns.

Nodal (834) who sat in blue and white robes, tall with dark skin, acted as head of this council and made firm decisions that overruled the others in a moment's notice. There was no majority vote, but his vote and the others complied or complained.

Also, I noticed clear communication was used when the age of each council member was placed after each name. They eluded much pride in their ages and I wanted to comply and not complain.

Also, I was taught to use these ages throughout my reports as distributor to bring smiles to all its citizens who reveled in old age connected to wisdom.

I stood in blue and black robes, but on our planet, they were not called blue and black, but for your understanding we will call them that.

I felt instant anxiety in standing before ten of the oldest individuals in the region. I knew they did not present me there to talk about the weather, which stayed a constant breezy and sunny comfortable temperature due to planetary machines.

THE MAN WHO DIDN'T WANT TO GO TO EARTH

They seemed to all block their thoughts because I could not sense a thing. I stared intently at my mother to get something from her, but it was not forthcoming. They all sat with slight smiles on their faces as if they knew all they needed to know. I someday wanted to be like them, *comfortable.*

(We are not comfortable by any means) my mother, Tonna picked up my thoughts (We have many stresses that are not perceived by the average individual, like how to keep the region safe from war)

(Is war imminent?) I thought, alarmed (The destroyers are dead. Did they make a comeback I am not aware of?)

Shuri (624) raised her wrinkled dark hand to calm my nerves. She smiled with calm white eyes and her white hair glistened from overhead lights (War is never imminent, but it can be averted. It is always on the horizon. What do you know about Earth?)

I stood for a moment, confused and turned from one to another as if it was a trick question.

(I know nothing about it and don't want to know anything about it. They are savages) I thought.

(They are no better or worse than we were over two-hundred long turns ago) my mother thought (We were perceived as savages by the Harmonic Aliens, and they helped us anyway with their technology and a few absorbed individuals and here we are. They can be saved from themselves)

THE MAN WHO DIDN'T WANT TO GO TO EARTH

(Why are you so concerned about Earthlings? Their technology is no match for ours. They wouldn't last a day against us) I thought, angered.

(Their technology has been enhanced since Mars returned to battle his daughters in their Earth year of 2085. All they did was use the scraps from destructive ships to move ahead almost two-hundred long turns) My mother thought.

(Crafty bastards) I thought (They still do not know how to use the wormhole. We have the codes to move in and out without problems) I thought.

(Yes, but how long?) Shuri asked (Already several committees are being formed to pressure the Phasees on Earth to give them the codes; but even if the Phasees do not relent and give them the codes they have several committees designed to find the codes on their own. We see ten long turns at the most)

I stood, silent in thought and looked from face to face, but could not figure what they wanted me to do about it.

(What do you want me to do?) I asked, but the clarification came from each of them as a deep thought (You want me to go there and be a distributor, to help them with goods and services and improve their life so they don't find a way through the wormhole and find us)

(We want you to be the great distributor you are and improve on their lives, yes) Juni (804) thought.

My mother leaned to him and thought secretly, but I could sense she chided him for using great...

THE MAN WHO DIDN'T WANT TO GO TO EARTH

(Okay, don't be great, be excellent. Is that a better word?) Juni asked with a smile of even white teeth.

(I don't want to be anything on that planet. I have no intention of going to that place) I thought (Push comes to shove and they find a way through the wormhole, you could collapse it

(Everybody knows the wormhole was manufactured by the Harmonic Aliens for better commerce connections. It will take them many long turns to get to us, by then we would be ready)

(Your suggestions are immature and based on fear and anger, Mr. Lin Jo) Nodal thought (That is why you are the best one for this mission. It will help you, us and them through the matter. You must see the long term of it)

They could sense I was not going to budge and ended the communication with a nod of their heads and smiles. I sensed something below the surface but could not detect what it was because they were masters in thought blocking/projecting, and I was not.

(Tell your brother, Abu I am thinking about him) my mother thought before the gray chamber doors were sealed and I stood for a moment in deep reflection.

Abu was my younger brother (120) and peered from northern Jan through the view screen. He had two sons and they played in the background and two of his companions waved and I responded with a wave and a smile; but we did not find that a distraction, because the noise of

22

THE MAN WHO DIDN'T WANT TO GO TO EARTH

children and family always brought comfort to Urbanites.

(It's a new opportunity for you. You should take it) he thought.

I then knew she had connected with him three short turns ago (2 and a half Earth days) and wanted him to butter me up to take the offer.

(I could never hide things from you brother. You were always faster when it came to thoughts than me) he thought.

(I'm no master. I just know how *you* think) I thought.

We both laughed and he patted his leg as he did in the past when something humorous was thought, then he stared at me intently.

(You have a deep fear of this planet Earth. Why?) he asked.

(It's a free will zone. Anything can happen. I don't like that. Here we have set restrictions) I thought.

(Be careful what you fear. It may come true) Abu stared, concerned.

(Not if I can help it) I thought, and my eyes dropped as my fear gradually became a reality.

THE MAN WHO DIDN'T WANT TO GO TO EARTH

2

(Written from Planet Jan)

My full name is Liman Jo, but several syllables fell off and I left it, without correction. Some called me Jo and others called me Li, I didn't care. With open thoughts in operation much was implied.

So, my name was in the title of this book (man), but as you can tell I am not a man, but from another place far away.

By the time I arrived on several planets as a distributor of goods my name changed to Lin and in time I was pegged as *the Great Distributor*, which left me uncomfortable.

In the word *great* there was no room for improvement. Only *God* was *Great,* but many friends and constituents were not trying to compare me to God, God Forbid, or equal to God, God Forbid...the horror.

They claimed they used the term affectionately and with deep respect; but it made me uncomfortable just the same.

I visited several planets in this solar system to help correct distribution problems before I became betrayer of the Great Can of Urb.

I did go to school for many planet rotations, almost ten Earth years in distribution of goods and services.

When many found my ideas could work, they began to implement them into society and many lives were improved.

THE MAN WHO DIDN'T WANT TO GO TO EARTH

I am 201 years young, but when the word *Great* began to be attached to my name, I wanted no parts of it and recused-myself on many fronts and remained in seclusion with my son Hut. This had a two-toned effect. First it protected me from the hands of Great Can who wanted retribution for the survival of hundreds of Fumans, which I initiated because I felt genocide of any species was wrong and it gave us privacy from the cameras and microphones of nosy inhabitants.

Many thought I was overreacting about the inclusion of great in my name, but I did not want hero worshippers and the evil that goes with it on my conscience.

My former female friend, Brie, exasperated by my seclusion, threatened to take Hut with her; but I challenged her to do so, it was a half/half connection with the young one.

She knew incarceration from certain authorities would commence immediately, because in our society a child's protection and growth was encouraged by both parents.

Brie smiled sadly on a visual screen that resembled reflected water, but was only electrons, stabilized to look like a communication device.

She had brown hair, a long forehead, front and back and beautiful prominent white eyes, which is what attracted me to her ten long turns ago.

After the birth of Hut (who was now 8), she decided to travel and gave me full rights, with some visitation rights on her end.

THE MAN WHO DIDN'T WANT TO GO TO EARTH

(You called my bluff) as her thoughts slowly moved through electrons.
She sighed deeply and looked down, crestfallen.
(He is well taken of) I thought, to calm her worries.
(Just be careful. Great Leader Can is on the lookout for the betrayers who turned against him in dealing with the rough men) she thought.
(Still, he searches. It's been several long cycles) I thought, alarmed.
(He doesn't let go easily) she thought. (I must go. I will contact Hut later so we can talk)
(He will be happy to hear from you) I thought as her image phased into darkness.

We are the betrayers.

There were five of us that helped Mars on planet Urb against Great Leader Can.
Jed, Shi, Lin (me), Pa and Tor. I looked at an electronic picture taken after the betraying. It only gave me images of a deep sadness that didn't go away.
The picture after the betrayal was close to nine Earth years, because my son was not born yet. I was still in the throes of getting to know my then partner, Brie.

I had been in deep contemplation lately and my son noticed this and was prepared to leave.
(No) I waved him in.
(I didn't want to disturb you) he carefully walked in and slanted his large head sideways (You are troubled)

THE MAN WHO DIDN'T WANT TO GO TO EARTH

I only nodded and hugged him for comfort. He was only nearly four feet high and wore white robes with yellow trims. His white eyes were prominent with dark skin that appeared thick, almost like scales, because he was not fully grown. This was the way of our species.

With prominent noses and thin lips, we almost resembled Phasees who were shorter with thick skins (receding scales).

There was not much difference between our species and the Fumans on Earth, which gave us some resemblance to Earthlings, despite our tall nature.

(I had been thinking about some things) I patted a nearby clear chair, as Hut carefully sat (I know we have not been traveling as we should. That is my fault. So, I propose an offer...)

(You want me to improve my scholar grades in school and you will put in for Earth travel! Yes...) Hut stood, with fists balled, triumphant.

(You must reach *excellent status*...) I thought.

Hut suddenly looked crestfallen and sat down, hard. I patted him on the leg, affectionately.

(That's wrong, father. No one barely achieves excellent status in academics...) he looked down, dejected.

(I did...) I countered.

He looked up, surprised.

(It took me several long rotations, but you are in a younger class. Your fight should last no more than two months at the most) I thought.

How wrong I was.

27

THE MAN WHO DIDN'T WANT TO GO TO EARTH

3

Pitta kept a dark secret from her daughter Nesh. Nesh was only nine long rotations (almost eight Earth years), but she was very sensitive and could go deep in thought and emotions quickly.

Pitta, in fear of her daughter knowing about her dark, bloody secret called in the emotion/thought blocker, Master Har, to train her in the "art of blocking." Better known on Earth as the "Blank Page Movement."

Their lessons usually resumed once a week, deep in the cycle turn before daylight and only if Nesh was deeply sleep. This went on for several long rotations, until Master Har could not sense an emotion or thought from Pitta.

When she paid him handsomely for his last session, he watched a long black device that beeped readily with galactic funds. When he smiled and stood, she smiled and stood, and they hugged gingerly.

Har was a tall Janeite from the planet Jan. Janeites were usually red in complexion in comparison to Urbanites who had a dark complexion, smaller head sizes and less prominent eyes.

Har stood back and patted her arms gently, pleased at her progress.

(I'm going to miss these sessions) he thought.

(You are always welcome to come by anytime) she smiled.

(I'm going to Earth in several short rotations. You are welcome to come with us) he thought.

THE MAN WHO DIDN'T WANT TO GO TO EARTH

(I have no desire to go there. Too much drama and death) she thought.

(Much improved in the last one-hundred and forty-three long cycles. I am going with a couple of friends on a business transaction. Lots of money involved. You can come as a security guard just in case things get dicey. We don't expect any problems, but this *is* Earth) he smiled deeply.

She could not assess anything from his smile because he was a master at thought/emotion blockages. She sighed deeply and considered...

(My daughter always wanted to visit Earth, but I am not so sure it is all that safe. Let me think about it. Who is all on board to go?) she asked.

(Char from Pro and Ilic from Phaes) he thought.

He suddenly felt a flood of emotions when he spoke the name *Ilic*. She felt slightly ashamed that she could not contain her emotions after her last session on how to block them.

(You will not be able to contain them forever. They are a part of you always, but to achieve subterfuge you need better discipline) he chastised.

She only nodded and bowed her head.

(May I try to surmise the situation?) he asked carefully.

She only nodded.

(He's not a lover, but an adversary. Something to deal with the rough man Mars. He tried to hijack a ship you were on, and you subdued him. His history is sketchy beyond that) he thought.

THE MAN WHO DIDN'T WANT TO GO TO EARTH

She looked up with a faint smile. He only smiled, pleased he pulled thoughts and emotions that were deep.
(There are many ships going to Earth. You don't have to take our ship, but it's the new Phaes, some call it Phaes 2) he thought.
(I want no parts of it) she thought.
(If you change your mind we will not leave for several short rotations) he thought.
She patted him on the arm, and he left. As the green door slid over and sealed, she leaned against it as her contained peace seemed to unravel under emotions pressed down.

Pitta was born on Pro but moved to Urb after ten long turns. Her parents traveled the skies and space, battling other planets as mercenaries and grew a large sum of funds from their ventures.
She grew up under constant pressure to perfect her fighting skills as they moved toward retirement, because "that was where the money and security was."
She rarely killed individuals, but there were times she was placed in unfortunate spots when she had to kill or be killed. This was the bloody secret she wanted to keep from her daughter.

Pitta wore a yellow and green robe as she moved about the food circle (kitchen) that resembled a circle encased in yellow and orange walls. Light moved about as Pitta shifted her focus and began to prepare a simple meal of green roughage and sao (a type of fish).

THE MAN WHO DIDN'T WANT TO GO TO EARTH

Nesh floated into the food circle and smiled at a soft landing. Pitta was pleased and ruffled her dark brown plaits.

(You are getting much better) Pitta thought (Prepare for your meal. Wash your arms and hands, Nesh).

They ate quietly for some time as smiles crossed the circled green table. With some windows open in a circular space outside noises of air cars and night creatures filtered into the quiet.

(Mother, I want to see the picture of father) she asked.

(You have seen it to death) she admitted, flabbergasted.

(I want to see it again, please) Nesh wiped her mouth with a green cloth.

(Okay) she moved her hand (There you go)

A large electronic picture floated above the table. Nesh smiled at the image of Mars who stared stoically with several behind him.

(You know who is standing behind him?) Pitta asked.

(You, along with Mr. Arn) she paused in thought.

(On Earth they call them *uncles*) she waved her hand and encouraged her to continue.

(Uncles?) she frowned at the thought (Ms. Ntb, his companion, Mr. Pun, Mr. Dawe, Ms. Sha, and Ms. Cantata)

Pitta made the picture go away with a wave of her hand. They sat in quiet contemplation for some time, until Nesh shattered her night with another request.

(I want to go to Earth, mother) Nesh thought.

31

Pitta only bowed her head and raised it to stare at her daughter, exasperated. Nesh sensed agitation from her and remained quiet and sensed the name: *Ilic.*

Pitta took some time to gather her thoughts as she pressed down thoughts of Ilic with little success.

(It takes half a long rotation to be acclimated or you can get sick and die) Pitta reminded.

(I know) Nesh contained her angst.

(There are hostiles everywhere and war is imminent) Pitta thought.

(That is no longer true since the Harmonics are in control) Nesh admitted.

Pitta had to admit this and nodded her head slowly.

(But Mar's grandson started a war with the world and it's on fire) she interjected.

(This is no longer true as Mars the younger paused his invasions to abide by the Harmonic's wishes) Nesh admitted.

Pitta stared, surprised. Nesh stared at her dark hands and tried to contain her ambitions. Pitta saw through the ruse.

(You have been studying with Hut so he could gain *excellent status*) Pitta thought (This had been going on for some time)

(Almost thirty short rotations) Nesh stared up at her mother (I would like us to go with him)

Pitta drank from a long glass, colored green and blue. She placed it down and pressed her thin tan lips together.

THE MAN WHO DIDN'T WANT TO GO TO EARTH

(That's a tall order to achieve excellent status and to keep someone else in the same) Pitta smiled weakly.

Nesh smiled at her mother.

(It's a challenge I take) Nesh agreed.

THE MAN WHO DIDN'T WANT TO GO TO EARTH

<u>4</u>

Pitta contacted me through the view screen and gave me a mischievous stare and smile. When she smiled like that, I knew I had been *used* and sat back to await any devastating news.

(It's not that bad) she leaned forward as electrons around her shifted in color (Prepare yourself for an *Earth Excursion*)

I blinked my white eyes rapidly and turned my head aside to think. I was still not up to par, and she emitted glee I could not *read* her.

(What do you know about my agreement with Hut?) I stared intently (I'm not getting a thing)

(My daughter Nesh is a class below him, but she is good at academia and had been schooling him) she smiled broadly.

(Why are you all aboard with this? I understood we were on a similar level when it came to Earth) I asked, intrigued.

(I'm doing it for Nesh. She wants to visit because she has not been there yet, curiosity, I suspect) she thought as her eyes dropped down.

I accepted her answer, but below the surface something boiled.

(The things we do for our young ones) I thought.

The adobe my son and I resided in was one level of shiny, green and blue floors that shimmered as if alive when walked on. Our furniture was simple sitting constructs long and short, beige and brown, with green-stemmed creatures that moved with the sunlight and became immobile as the sun declined.

THE MAN WHO DIDN'T WANT TO GO TO EARTH

With only a short rotation at night things moved quickly into slumber mode as the sun dropped away. I walked pass Hut's room of view screens, dark-colored walls and calm lights. He sat with legs crossed, suspended by mental thought as his eyes darted from one image to another.

I stood and observed his quick reaction as each image from Earth came in short stories.

(You may enter, father) he thought.

I knew it was proper to wait at the door and enter only when asked as a form of respect. I stepped behind him and watched the images and smiled.

(History lesson?) I asked.

(A little history can go a long way) he admitted with a smile.

(You are still in World War 2. You have a way to go) I thought.

(Only a short time. When the atomic bomb hit things changed for Humanity quickly) he thought.

I nodded my head. He was right.

We four stood in the Preparation Center for Planet Visitation (PCPV) which resided in the center of Planet Jan. It was a large facility that was interconnected by underground tunnels and secret doors. I trembled to think what could reside underground.

I was pleased our rooms were above ground and well lit. Thirty other containers were in our room. A few other individuals stood from other worlds (Pro and Urb) and received instructions on how to take the injections.

Shal was a tall Jan with red skin and dark robes and moved about with grace as he tried to allay any fears.

(Side effects) I thought.
(Vomiting, dizziness, dry skin, which can cause skin breakage and bleeding, because we are thick-skinned. If it continues, we stop treatments and disband the whole thing) Shal thought glumly.
(Let's hope that does not happen) I thought.
I was surprised when I felt fingers in mine. When I looked over it was Pitta. I did not expect this type of affection from her, she was usually thick-skinned, tough.
She stood a foot taller than I and our look as a couple appeared odd on the surface, if we were together.
(This does not mean we are together) she thought.
I did not suspect we were. Usually, eight long rotations (almost 9 Earth years) had to occur before a couple was considered serious. There was no ceremony, just the knowledge to know they were together.

With so many things happening to the body we are placed in stasis as the chemicals were introduced. Our tube was darkened to block out light so we could sleep or meditate.
I had preferred to meditate but a dream moved into my thoughts and began to take form. I had no control over it and observed things as if from above.

...My son ran quickly as I hurried him along and looked behind us at something...Whatever it was had two heads, was large and stomped about looking for us...

THE MAN WHO DIDN'T WANT TO GO TO EARTH

I suddenly was awake as the tube parted and allowed light to filter into the room. Shal walked about thinking calming thoughts as he instructed us to lie still for a time. I heard vomiting sounds. Shal gave the vomiters a tube to use as their bile moved quickly away from their space into a chute underneath the floor.

(Juice to settle your stomach has been included in your tube) Shal thought (You will be raised, slowly) we were raised slowly until we were upright (Collect yourselves)

I turned and noticed Pitta who appeared sleepy. When I raised my hand, in a wave, nausea struck me, and I used the tube just in time. I also saw Hut and Nesh get violently ill.

(Weaklings) Pitta thought.

I wanted to laugh, but nausea overwhelmed me, and I used the tube once again.

It took many of us some time to gather ourselves and Shal was a calming force. Only five of us (including Pitta) did not receive side effects; but I was much disturbed that the young ones became sick. There were three (counting our young ones) an older young one, about twelve.

I suddenly gestured Shal into a near corner for privacy, but on a planet of mind readers the only ones safe were blank pagers.

(I had a strange experience while under) I thought.

(The chemicals can alter your mind cohesion, which is your sane/insane center. You can see things that are not there. Feel things that are not happening) Shal patted my shoulder to end

THE MAN WHO DIDN'T WANT TO GO TO EARTH

the thoughts of craziness (Within a week if it continues, we will stop the treatments) (It will only disappoint my son) I thought. (Your health is more important) Shal reminded.

I stood outside in dimness as overhead lights began to automatically brighten. A wind began to pick up and our robes flapped a little. (Moisture from the skies, shortly) Hut admitted.

(We had better get back) I thought and reached to shake Pitta's hand, but she hugged me instead.

(You hung in there. You are not as weak as I thought you were) she thought.

I did not feel slighted in the sense. I felt she was having fun at my expense, but I didn't mind. I could take a joke.

(I don't feel like going back home, yet) Pitta turned to her daughter and smiled (You are thinking what I am thinking?)

(We should crash the party) Nesh thought with a smile.

(If you don't mind us crashing?) Pitta asked.

(Not at all) I looked at Hut who stared, just as surprised as I was.

THE MAN WHO DIDN'T WANT TO GO TO EARTH

5

Ilic was more upset that his name was mispronounced and misspelled than the fact he was in a pressurized case against a former business partner.

Har sat behind him in a highchair to show his authority over Char, his assistant and Ilic. Har sometimes reminded them they were helpers, and he oversaw the whole plan to make a lot of funds through solar system interchange.

Char was born on Pro to parents Lua and Shen Ta. He was an only child who had a bright pale complexion and as he matured gravitated toward gambling ventures where he gained more funds than he lost.

When Har came along with a business proposition to make a lot of money on Earth Char jumped at the chance.

Har knew what he was doing when he asked Char along for the ride. He knew Char had been on Earth briefly during the Superhuman Invasion of 2153, when he was slightly hurt in the leg, he abandoned Earth for other ventures on Mars and Venus, which had a lower population and less violence.

Char returned to Earth only to be near the Giant Feet invasion of 2171 where he was injured in the arm. He vowed not to return to Earth but rescinded that promise when Har gave him a proposition of glory and money.

(Who cares about them mispronouncing your name, Ilic? You are being hunted by the

THE MAN WHO DIDN'T WANT TO GO TO EARTH

Authoritarians and this places a dangerous element in our plan to get rich) Har argued.

(Also, don't forget the fact that you have a search and destroy against you from Great Leader Can, for the betrayer incident) Char pointed out.

Ilic pointed furiously.

(That was a misunderstanding. I helped Great Can hold the rough men at bay. It's not my fault if he couldn't contain them) Ilic thought.

(We must go into hiding until we can figure out what our next move will be. Let's go to the closest place with fine accommodation. Let's go to Jan or Pro, Urb is filled with several authority forces looking for you, Ilic) Har thought.

(Let's flip on it) Char thought with a smile.

(You like to flip on everything) Ilic thought, irritated.

(It solves a lot of problems) Char produced a rounded object that shimmered with touch.

Har appeared bored so Char picked sides for Pro or Jan.

(Jan it is) Ilic thought.

Pitta was pleased when she and her daughter "crashed the party," a term used in Jan to indicate when guesses arrived unexpectedly and could stay for an extended time.

She also wanted to see if there was a spark between her and Lin. She was not so sure. They did not seem to click on many fronts, but he was quiet, nice and neat. She was used to rugged individuals.

Also, being an outsider and guest, she did her research and knew they could accommodate them with the four sleep rooms, spacious food

THE MAN WHO DIDN'T WANT TO GO TO EARTH

circle (kitchen) and hefty living area space (living room).
Nesh received her own room of green and beige walls, brown flooring and clear furniture.
Pitta was slightly startled to see Lin before she sensed his presence. He backed away from the door and she waved him in.
(My senses are dull, or I would have noticed you ahead of time) she thought.
(I hope that's because you feel comfortable at my place) he thought.
(That must be it) she thought with humor.
His pointed eyebrows rose in surprise. She gestured for him to sit in a clear chair.
(I do have some sense of humor) she thought with a wry smile.
(Rarely used) Lin thought.
She suppressed a smile, then stared more seriously.
(You have something dire on your mind) she surmised.
He exhaled deeply before he stared with white eyes.
(Did you have any dreams before coming from the treatment?) he asked.
He could tell she held something in, but it was hard to tell with blockages in place. The word *Ilic* rose and filtered away like ash in the wind.
(Who is Ilic?) he asked.

He knew the rules on picking up images and emotions from another and knew she had the right not to respond. When she did not but stared with angst he nodded and asked about any dreams under treatment.

THE MAN WHO DIDN'T WANT TO GO TO EARTH

(It made no sense. I don't know what the dream was trying to tell me. We were all on a ship going to Earth and we were struck by another ship, then I emerged out of treatment) she replied.
He only nodded.
(In mine my son and I were being chased by a creature with large teeth, two heads and eight feet tall, terrifying) he thought.
(Oh my. You know it's natural to experience night terrors, even hallucinations during the treatments) she admitted.
(I suddenly don't feel alone in my dreaming) he thought.

(Did you dream during the treatment?) I asked Hut who sat next to Nesh as they played visual games.
Visual games were a form of video games, but with thought and emotion connected with visuals to form events like a picture. Nesh moved her hand and destroyed Hut's battleship. He stared at me, disappointed. Then paused the game.
(Thanks father) he thought.
(Sorry. I need an answer. I am gathering information on dream state and treatments) I thought as I sat down in a clear chair.
(There are several articles and volumes written on the matter of individuals who saw things in dream state, and they came true. They were considered prophetic dreams) he mentally pushed images to my view screen (I did the research ahead of time. It's not promising)
(Why do you think that?) I asked, alarmed.
(Some disturbing information about the side effects, which can cause hallucinations, and

THE MAN WHO DIDN'T WANT TO GO TO EARTH

insanity. In some instances, there was prophetic dreaming. You are not thinking about backing out, are you?) he asked.
(No, of course not) I floundered on my stand, and I am sure he sensed it.
(Well, I had a bad dream) he paused in reaction.
(What kind of dream?) I asked.
(I was being chased by a creature with two heads) he admitted.
It felt like cold water was sprayed on my warm body. I stood unsteadily. He noticed my reaction.
(You had the same dream. I don't think it's prophetic. Never heard of a creature with two heads) he thought.
(Yes) I agreed.
I looked slowly at Nesh, and she frowned, because she sensed the question beforehand.
(I dreamt of a ship hitting our ship. That's not the same dream) she admitted.
I only nodded and left them to their visual games, fearful of the similarities.

Ilic sat in a long room with yellow and green walls, a food center and washroom accommodations. He moved images with his hand, because his mind was too filled with stress to do anything right.
When his former partner's face (Geta) appeared on his visual screen. Ilic became instantly agitated.
Geta was a short Urbanite (6 feet even) and sat in black robes with green stripes. He wore white

garbs wrapped around his head that shifted as he moved his long head.
(Finally, I have you) Geta glared with white eyes (How long have we been friends? Thirty long rotations? And you treat me thus. You steal my invention)
(It is our design and construct, not only yours) Ilic thought firmly.
His eyes narrowed and Ilic could feel anger and betrayal that emanated from him (Let's meet somewhere private) he pushed mentally.
(So, you can hand me over to Great Leader Can and obtain the reward? You need more practice in hiding your thoughts. Your class in subterfuge is not paying off, so far) Ilic thought.
Geta hissed between his white-even teeth and looked downward. Then he stared up, undefeated.
(You stole my project) he glared.
(Our project) Ilic corrected (You had intentions of going it alone with Har, but I beat you to it. You really need to work on hiding your intentions better. Also, you tried to impose violent images on the beasts, while I wanted them docile, easy to tame) Ilic thought.
(Who said I didn't do it already? How would you know, unless you know where to look?) he asked.
Ilic felt like someone dumped cold water on him, but it was the cold of fear as he realized he was never fully in control of his own project.
(Some way you will pay. You will see) Geta thought, then blanked the screen.

THE MAN WHO DIDN'T WANT TO GO TO EARTH

Ilic felt uneasy with the threat and was pleased he was not before a view screen to be noticed in his fear.

He soon stood before the project and began to look at several screens to find a glitch to tell him it was tampered with, but it all seemed all right. When Har stood behind him, he relished in the anxieties of his friend.

(He probably didn't do a thing. He's messing with your head) Har thought with a green cup of rejuvenation in his hand.

(He had this obsession with Earth wars, especially the Superhuman invasion of 2153 and the Giant Feet invasion of 2171, but I don't see anything of that sort here) Ilic moved screens around, frantic.

(He has obsessions because he was at both events) Har thought.

Ilic turned to him, surprised.

(I didn't know that) Ilic thought.

(Well, if he did put it on there, he would not place it so that it can be found. We can vet it on Earth in a secure area. Can't let that slow our progress down) Har growled and walked away.

Ilic only sighed and dropped his head, defeated for now.

THE MAN WHO DIDN'T WANT TO GO TO EARTH

6

As the treatments continued, we still had bizarre dreams, but they all appeared jumbled thoughts, nothing prophetic.

At times I could feel the pride that poured from my son as he noticed I intended to go through with the treatments until the end.

Of course, I had my reservations; but wanted to push through for him and Nesh, his close friend.

By the seventh medium rotation (near six Earth weeks) many of the side effects of the mixture began to lessen. I felt confident that things were about to turn about, until view screen events exposed a hunt for the five betrayers in Jan.

(You can't let that stop our fun) Pitta thought.

I turned to her, then turned back to the screens in the family room. I had positioned three wide screens close to each other for full sound and visual effects.

(The betrayers, us five, now six with Ilic) she displayed discomfort with his name (Our faces are now all over the planet. We will have to escape as soon as we find a way) I thought.

(That's stopping our fun) Pitta frowned.

(I never thought I would agree to this, but we may have fun when we reach Earth) I smiled wryly.

She smiled too and noticed my sarcasm in play.

(You don't believe that at all) she thought.

(It's all for the little ones) I thought (Electronic tickets in the ready?)

THE MAN WHO DIDN'T WANT TO GO TO EARTH

(Don't need an electronic ticket, like Jan, Pro or Urb) she thought.
(No electronic travel tickets?) I asked.
(It's not monetized) she thought.
(Not yet give it time) I thought.
(We will head back to my adobe for a time until the initial liftoff) she thought with a smile (I see you want to meet with the other betrayers, be careful, please)
(I will. I need to see what their game plan is. It may help us) I thought.

I sat in a small enclosure under sediments of stone and rock in dim lights around a long table made from rock and other sediments.
Various colors of your Earthly blue, grey and quartz shimmered with our movement as we drank hot liquid of orange and green.
There were five of us: Jed, Shi, Pa, Tor (better known as "To" on other planets), and me. Shi was the leader among us, just as she was on Urb against the rough men, who we were sent to spy on, but helped in the last minute due to me "growing a conscience."
Shi had a long head covered by gold-colored hair with fine garments of green and blue that appeared worn. She was used to fine things and the nine years hiding from death took its toll. It said in her face.
(So, we are the five, betrayers) she thought.
I could feel the angst and remorse that poured from her small frame. Tor, Jed, and Pa stiffened their frames as they felt her emotions.

THE MAN WHO DIDN'T WANT TO GO TO EARTH

(Just because you grew a conscience, Lin, here we all sit. I had a partner and four sons at home, but that didn't matter to you) she thought.

(I've been married for one-hundred and thirty-two years, with twenty-two young ones and eight grandchildren, but I get to see none of them) Pa thought, angered as he pressed his dark, hard fingers together.

(I miss my significant other. We just became partners after seven long turns. I know the initial going rate is eight long turns, but we can make it work) Tor thought, with hope (If I return home)

(Can't do that with Great Leader Can and his son rounding up citizens. You return home you place your loved ones in danger) Jed admitted.

(So far, we are safe if we keep a low profile and rarely go out, but in subterfuge, under disguise, check if we are being followed, or not) Shi demanded to Jed.

When Jed rose and left, we all sat in silent meditation in our own thoughts until his return.

(It doesn't look like we were followed) Pa thought.

There were sighs about the table as we saw our lives flash before our eyes, because we suspected they would take no prisoners.

(We are hidden in these rock formations, almost underground and have our own lighted source) Shi broke the silent moment.

(Unfortunately, it's a matter of time before they find us. We may have to go to another planet, like Pro to regroup and begin again) I thought.

THE MAN WHO DIDN'T WANT TO GO TO EARTH

(Or another planet like Earth?) Shi asked, slyly.

I suddenly felt uncomfortable as white eyes stared, surprise and betrayal poured from each of them.

(It's just a short vacation. I promised my son) I admitted.

(You had no intentions of returning to your usual adobe after your vacation. You were going to go hide in Pro. When were you going to tell us about your new plan?) Shi asked.

It was evident that Shi probed quicker and deeper than the others. This came from mistrust, and I did not blame her one bit.

(After my return from Earth) I admitted, reluctantly.

She only nodded as the others made disappointing sounds through their mouth and nose.

(We agreed to keep each other informed) Tor thought, angered.

(I would have informed you all on my return. I don't think we can stay here much longer) I thought.

(We are safe) Shi emphasized.

I did not want to argue with her. I could feel their volatile emotions and knew it was a matter of time before they completely turned on me.

(Look) I stood and raised my hands palms out as a sign of surrender (I know you did not introduce this life, but look at it from the other end, we saved over hundreds of bodies that almost became fodder for the fields. We don't know how

THE MAN WHO DIDN'T WANT TO GO TO EARTH

the remaining Fumans advanced; but we gave them a chance at life. That's enough for me)
(Not for me) Shi quickly responded.
I only nodded and looked around the table as they appeared to agree with her, but that was the surface. Pa did not want to go along with the violence but pretended too for his own safety.
(We can talk about this when I return) I thought.
I quickly exited through a sliding side door and wondered if I would make it to my flying vehicle of green and black. When I coasted above the rocks and sediment the other betrayers emerged to look up in dim rays from a falling sun.

THE MAN WHO DIDN'T WANT TO GO TO EARTH

7

(He seems to believe he is going on vacation) Shi turned to Lin's rising ship (Hate to obstruct his plans)

(We should have tried for him in the meeting area. This way is more reckless) Jed thought with angst.

(No, it's a perfect plan. We keep blood off our hands) she thought.

(There is no such thing as a perfect plan and the blood will still be on our hands) Jed glared at her.

Shi tried not to stare at his stern eyes and nervously stared skyward.

(I don't see an explosion) Pa thought.

(Wait for it) she thought.

Lin communicated with the ship before takeoff about hidden contraptions. He knew Jed had to leave to check the skies for Great Leader Can aircraft. When he returned Lin felt deception from him.

(The bomb materials have been removed) the ship communicated in a thick tone.

(Let's hurry home, quickly) Lin thought, worried.

The ship banked left and took off at quick speed, while the four betrayers watched, amazed their plan was a dud.

(Nothing happened) Jed grumbled and glared at Shi.

(He saw through my ruse to check the skies. We must stop him from going to Earth, *now*) Jed glared at each betrayer, then walked off.

THE MAN WHO DIDN'T WANT TO GO TO EARTH

(We need to start packing) Lin encouraged his son as he watched Earth Events Channel. (Already packed and ready) Hut could feel the angst from his father. He leaned from the clear chair and stared intently.
(Something wrong?) Hut asked.
(We need to go, *now*) Lin thought as he touched buttons as silver bags moved forward (Already packed myself)
(We need to inform Nesh and her mother we are leaving early) Hut thought.
(Already there) I thought as a view screen emerged and Pitta's image appeared (We need to go, *now*)
She nodded and darkened the screen.

Tor adjusted weapons and flash bombs on his waist. He lingered until he could not linger any longer.
He was not up to the violence that was about to ensue, but he had to go along or risk instant death, because he was not trained to hide his emotions and thoughts.
(You are taking too long, Tor. What is the hold-up?) Jed asked.
(I'm ready) Tor thought, but emotionally he was not.
They hurried to a waiting air vehicle brown-colored with pointed spikes on each end. When it rose with Shi as flyer and Pa in the back passenger seat, angst filled the vehicle.
Tor and Pa exchanged looks and they fell in sync to the matter this was not what they planned or wanted to participate in.

52

THE MAN WHO DIDN'T WANT TO GO TO EARTH

As the four betrayers landed their aircraft it was near daylight. Tor stayed back to steer the ship out in case of trouble as the others made their way forward with weapons ready.

(Watch your fire with the little ones) Shi thought (The rough man girl and her son is staying with him as a *party crasher*)

There were certain sighs from various positions as some were not sure how to handle little ones in violence.

(I am no young-one killer) Shi admitted.

(Also, Pitta whipped the rough man so that he used a cane until his death. We can't take her lightly) Pa nodded from his position (True story)

The other three shook their heads negatively, knowing the story was probably embellished.

(I'm going in) Jed announced (Watch for counter fire)

Pa, and Shi aimed their long, green weapons from different positions. Jed hurried forward and leaned on the wall and peered inside a wide window. It appeared dark inside.

(I don't know if they are home) Jed touched a flat knob and didn't expect it to open, when it did, he was surprised…

An explosion erupted from the adobe that incinerated Jed's tall body. He barely had time to scream as the others fell, shocked, and traumatized.

Debris fell as the fire burned in several directions. Shi crawled away and dragged her weapon like a strange object that was too heavy.

THE MAN WHO DIDN'T WANT TO GO TO EARTH

Pa crawled to her position as Tor adjusted the ship so that it parked further away.
(I think we were, *had*) Tor thought.
(More than that, Jed is dead) Pa thought, near tears.
Shi forced herself to stand and leaned on her weapon for support.
(We need to get somewhere and rest, regroup and get this asshole) Shi thought.

(Ah, what the hell was that?) Faro looked through electronic eyes that zoomed (It looks like an intense light)
(It's a fire) Tonie, his sister admitted as she looked through electronic eyes (We should investigate)
(Not much happening here) Tepa, his brother thought (We should see what that is about. It appears bomb related)
Faro's gray eyebrows rose in interest.

As the sun's rays lit up the area, fire still burned in various spots as Faro's aircraft landed. Twenty silver tall robots with red eyes moved off with their hands raised as weapons.
Faro took a deep breath and took in the smoldered fire. When he closed his eyes as if he was in ecstasy, Tonie pushed past, irritated by the hold-up. Tepa shook his head negatively from the rear.
(Just enjoying the fire and cinders) Faro thought (Let's move in, carefully)
Robots scanned a body that was still burning, and they extinguished the flames so they could get a proper scan of its identity.

54

THE MAN WHO DIDN'T WANT TO GO TO EARTH

(Crispier and crispier) Tonie thought.

(It is the remains of Jed Lu of Urb) Robot 290 surmised.

(Betrayer Jed Lu) Faro thought (Fan out and look for clues to what happened here. We found one we can find the others)

When the explosion erupted Lin looked through his ships' visual in a secret place high in the atmosphere. When he sat back his eyes began to tear.

He saw Pitta in a far corner who noticed his distress and regret. She understood and nodded her head in silent agreement as Nesh and Hut smiled, they were finally going to *Earth*.

THE MAN WHO DIDN'T WANT TO GO TO EARTH

8

Jed's dark face and long nose came across information screens of his death. All citizens were connected to a network and when their life signs ceased information traveled to all the planets.

Of course, to receive this information you had to be tied to the network and requested such information, but it stung just the same, because I was involved in some way.

I sat, devastated. I had never taken another life before, but I used tactics schooled by Pitta, who was a master at martial arts, and covert operations.

I was hoping never to have to use it, but my hope was not enough. I sat with my eyes downcast for a time as Pitta stared from a far point. I sensed she wanted to give me space and I respected her for that decision.

(I'm going to lie down for a time) I suddenly stood.

Hut and Nesh turned from their open plans for Earth and Hut asked was I okay?

(Sure) I sighed deeply (Tired, that's all. Moving at slow speed for one rotation should take us to the wormhole)

Hut and Nesh stared, suspicious.

(I will watch the ship) Pitta suddenly was at my side (You rest)

(Someone died) Hut suddenly stood, alarmed, but I walked away before he could retain more information.

I did lay in a far back room under a dim light that turned above the small bed. It was in a dimly

THE MAN WHO DIDN'T WANT TO GO TO EARTH

lit room with view screens and wide windows and gray walls and laid away from the others for a while.

(It's obvious your best colors are gray and tan) she thought from the door.
I waved her in. I assumed that was the end of my private space. She wanted to communicate, and I did not want to deny that.
She sat on the edge of my bed as the door closed. I was surprised she would stay in a room with the door closed, with me.
(We already did the *party crasher* scene; I think we may be ready for the next best thing, but first you must tell me about Hut's mom, Brie. I can get bits of information from you, or you can tell me outright, why it failed?) she thought.
I tried to form my thoughts into one cohesive sentence.
(We went too fast) I thought.
She only nodded.

(The going rate is eight long rotations before sex for a strong relationship. This is scientific studies; they have been proven right, but there are cases when some have lasted over one hundred very long rotations after five long rotations before sex) she thought.
(There are exceptions. We thought we were the exception; but we fell into scientific examples. After intense sex of one long rotation, she wanted to travel again, then she was pregnant, and it placed a dampening on her plans) I thought.
(She could have aborted the baby through thought) she admitted.

THE MAN WHO DIDN'T WANT TO GO TO EARTH

These thoughts made me uneasy, and she felt my unease.

(Sorry, that was insensitive of me) she admitted.

(It's okay, but I would have never known my son Hut if she aborted him. I talked her down and said I would take care of him while she traveled and made money) I thought.

(She's like a travel agent and she goes on planet excursions to answer questions the customers may have) she thought.

(Good money in that, especially since Earth is an open field in that direction) I admitted.

(So, the feelings you have for her are like a close friend) she pointed out.

(Something like that) I thought.

She touched my hand and suddenly deep kissed me. I was pleasantly surprised, and it showed on my face.

9

Char was 135 long rotations in longevity, but these were young in Pro standards. He sat forward as he flipped an object that was thick with writings imprinted in the factory.

He had black hair that was curly and covered his long head and short ears. He had skin that was thick and pink with scales below the surface. His white eyes narrowed as he stared at a small view screen that floated chest level.

(That's not good) Char thought.

Ilic stared down at his screen, oblivious to his surroundings, when he looked up, he saw Char's stare.

(What?) Ilic asked.

(Sending you the visual) Char pushed a button.

Ilic stared and sighed. Har walked from the back room and stared back and forth.

(One of Ilic's friends is dead) Har surmised.

(He was not my friend. I never met him) Ilic thought and seemed far away mentally.

(The death of Jed Lu intensified the investigation into the whereabouts of the five betrayers) Char read.

(Now six) Har thought.

Ilic stared upward, agitated.

(I have five sons at home and three companions. I have no time for this) Char thought.

(How do you have time for anything with five sons and three companions?) Har asked.

Char sighed and raised his eyebrows in protest. Har ignored the protest to get serious as Ilic shook his head from side to side.

THE MAN WHO DIDN'T WANT TO GO TO EARTH

(We cannot stay. We must move) Ilic stood abruptly.

(We go when I say we go) Har stared with hard eyes (I oversee this operation. I am about the money. If we leave too early, we could have our cargo confiscated, and we wouldn't want that, would we?)

(If we leave too late, we may end up dead) Char thought (Let's toss on it) he flipped a rounded object.

(No flip. We wait) Har walked away, finished with the communication.

(Then we flip?) Char asked.

Ilic turned to Char who smiled slyly and stared at a floating communication screen of dark colors.

Great Leader Can's face filled Faro's view screen. Great Can was born on Pro but traveled to Urb over eighty long turns ago and quickly moved up the ranks in power and authority.

The Elder Council had their reservations about electing an outsider but admitted there was no law (which they designed) on Urb against electing outsiders to the Authoritarian Seat.

They also knew if he moved outside their idea of a leader for Urb they could remove him with a vote.

His white eyes stared, blazoned with unforgiveness. His pink skin seemed flushed from overhead lights, but it was his anger that affected his physical look.

Faro saw the look before and knew he wanted retribution. Faro resembled his father,

THE MAN WHO DIDN'T WANT TO GO TO EARTH

except for the broad face and pressed white eyes that looked unhappy.

(Faro, *remember*) Can thought.

(I know, you want to be there after we catch the betrayers) Faro thought.

(Don't forget that Ilic one and that rough girl who had his baby) Can tried to remember her name.

(Her name is Pitta) Tepa admitted as he stood further back with long arms crossed (She is nowhere to be found. Last noticed in Pro shopping for infant clothes nine long rotations ago)

(She is originally from Pro, but I doubt if she will go back. We have ships in every sector, searching. Maybe she went to Earth. Find her for me. Maybe I can persuade her to act as my assistant or something) he smiled slyly.

When he darkened the screen Faro sat back to rest his nerves as Tepa made a sucking noise of displeasure.

(He doesn't want her for an assistant. We all know what he wants her for) Tepa thought.

(It is his wish that he wants her. We cannot argue the point) Faro typed in commands to Authoritative Sentries (Let the sentries find her. I have enough to do looking for the betrayers)

(The sentries will leave nothing for father if she resists, remember she whipped the rough man almost to death. Let me search and find her. It will be my special project) Tepa thought.

Faro felt deceit from his brother and turned to him with eyes that glared. He rescinded the sentries' new commands and gave those orders over to Tepa in electron colors and lights.

(She is for father, *only*) Faro thought.

THE MAN WHO DIDN'T WANT TO GO TO EARTH

(I know) Tepa thought.

When Tepa walked from the room Faro turned to the view screen and gave Can an update on Pitta.

(Tepa wants to find her for you) Faro admitted.

Caro looked irritated and turned his head upward in frustration.

(You should not have given him that project. You know he is unable to keep his member in his pants) Can thought.

(He wants to help, father. Let him help) Faro thought.

Can cursed quietly and fumed in his anger.

(Let him find her then you go in and take charge) Can commanded.

(Good plan) Faro agreed.

Deep down Faro wanted nothing to do with the rough girl situation. He had his taste of the rough men in the battle that ensued over nine long rotations ago.

Near one-hundred thirteen Urbanites died and over three hundred and forty-one Fumans were killed. He knew the exact count because he was made to bury the dead by his father as a punishment for losing the rough men, who escaped by the five betrayers and their ships.

The day of that battle still haunted him in quiet places of reflection. This search was more about redemption for him than following orders for the sake of receiving retribution.

Tonie's face appeared above his head with eyes filled with excitement.

THE MAN WHO DIDN'T WANT TO GO TO EARTH

(We found a signature in the area, and it looks to be enough to track) Tonie admitted.
(Be there shortly) Faro stood, pleased progress was achieved.

Faro stood further back as his sister, Tonie scanned the atmosphere and images began to flicker in and out of focus. She lightly cursed between pursed, blue lips (painted) and blinked white eyes that looked up.
(This is when Mr. Lin Jo arrived in an air car, then he left with Hut, cute kid, then they left in short turn) she thought.
Faro nodded and peered at the images that looked like ghosts.
(The other betrayers arrived, probably to finish Mr. Lin off...then, boom) she moved the scanner (Here it gets weak, because I cannot tell...where they went) she thought.
Faro looked disturbed and impatient.
(So, you got me out here for what?) he asked.
(Don't jump on me. This stuff is complicated. You must test the air, water) she thought.
(Do you have anything *more* for me?) he asked.
(Maybe a little something) she admitted.
(Good. What is it?) he asked.
She walked a few steps and motioned a roving sentinel away as she scanned. She whistled when she found it.
(Barely distinguishable) she thought.
The images of Shi, Tor and Pa came in and out of focus. Then it dissipated as they parted ways.

THE MAN WHO DIDN'T WANT TO GO TO EARTH

(Just enough to find one of them) Tonie admitted.

Faro faintly smiled and walked away, satisfied.

10

I woke from a long sleep (about a medium rotation) and found us close to the wormhole, but we needed a few days of acclimation before we wanted to push through.

Other ships moved in and out of the wormhole and there had been crashes in the past so beacon lights with embedded signals were placed in various spots so that ships did not collide.

I was not sure what was the science of placing these beacons in various spots, but if the ship was not fitted to follow certain patterns a crash was imminent.

Don't use them at your own peril.

Hut sat with Nesh as they pointed at ships as they moved past and disappeared in light and energy.

(We are far away from protruding ships that it will not cause a catastrophic incident) I thought.

(That wouldn't be a good vacation) Pitta sat down and watched the view screens.

(Hopefully the *Authoritarian Sentinels* will not search this far out for a few betrayers) I thought.

(You hope) Pitta responded.

(We should go now, just in case) Hut thought, worried.

(No, no, cannot rush the medicinal procedure, or we could get sick and die. They don't have Urb doctors on Earth) I thought.

Hut appeared bored and watched the time on his wrist. Nesh patted his arm and smiled at him.

(You can do this) she encouraged.

THE MAN WHO DIDN'T WANT TO GO TO EARTH

(Let's go and watch *Earth Channel* in the back room) he thought, defeated.

As they rose to leave, I smiled and waved at them as Pitta stood next to me.

(They match) she said.

I looked at her with wild eyes, surprised. She understood my look.

(Not that, they are good friends. Too young for all that) she thought with a wave of both hands.

(Six more long turns and they will be eligible for partner connections) I thought.

(I dread the day) she thought.

(One partner connection is enough for me) I thought as I sat down to stare at ships on monitors.

She sat next to me and seemed to hesitate in her words.

(You don't want to try partner connections again?) she asked.

(No, partner connections are a lot like matrimony on Earth, it doesn't work. We make promises we cannot keep, and it becomes a big mess in the end) I thought.

She sighed and I turned to her, surprised at her reaction.

(It's hard to read you since your blockage training. Don't tell me you want to try partner connections again) I asked.

(Never was connected by a partner in the legal sense) she thought.

(The rough man) I reminded her.

(No legal backing, just a night partner sponsored by his want to be companion, Ntb. He really fixed me. I didn't see it coming) she pouted in anger.

THE MAN WHO DIDN'T WANT TO GO TO EARTH

(He manipulated his cells to impregnate you quickly) I thought.
She looked surprised.
(What do you know about the process?) she asked.
(The ancients infused the rough men with a certain power to manipulate their body to go beyond its set system) I thought.
(Well, I did get something good out of it, despite the deception, my daughter, Nesh) she thought.
(She is a wonder) I thought with a smile.
When she touched my hand, it felt warm and tender. I was surprised by this move and since it was hard to read her, I had to guess.
(We should stay within the bounds of eight long cycles before we become intimate) I thought.
(Who cares? We already have five long cycles under our belt) she replied as she kissed my small dark ear.
(I do) I admitted.
When she rose and stared down at me like I bug I was sure she was going to crush me like one, but her hands rose in frustration. I sighed, satisfied she didn't pound me into submission.

11

Tepa liked to stand back with arms crossed and observe while others did the research. He had numerous female connections who tolerated his presence because of the riches they could ensue from his abundance, given by his father Great Can.

In the past Tepa had approached females with a strong arm, and at times he was known to rape a few, but through the protection of his father he was never condemned to death as per Urb Law.

This gained him many enemies in Urb Councils, which pushed to banish relations working alongside the leaders, but; Can, seeing the handwriting on the wall, blocked a few votes to protect his son.

Tepa also knew deep down he had no intentions of handing over his findings when it came to Pitta, whom he had a growing obsession for.

He wanted to keep her for himself in competition against his father, who always seemed to get what he wanted, when it came to his desires. To the Great Leader: "she was the one who got away."

Some saw Tepa's aggressiveness toward the females as his competition against his father, where he felt inadequate in matters of the opposite sex, but most saw him as a lowlife who wanted to dominate.

With two communicators and information finders and view screens Tepa felt he was in good hands even though he was not the one doing the work. This was his way of delegating authority.

THE MAN WHO DIDN'T WANT TO GO TO EARTH

Tepa and two communicator/information specialists stood in a dimly lit area that curved like a saucer and appeared to block light from the Central Sun.
Eons ago, Urbanites found the sun exposed many of their circuits and images to intense waves that eradicated many of the systems and devised a way to block the sunlight to protect their systems, through a System Shade like a dark tint, almost like Earth sunglasses.

Shoad, stood tall with a tan complexion. She was an Urb female with blue hair and white eyes. She turned to Tepa from several view screens as her green and black robe swayed.
(We seem to have found an image of Pitta) she thought.
(Show me) he ordered, as his body tensed.
Images came over the view screen almost larger than life as Pitta climbed in a gray air car with a female child and the ship moved into the stars.
(They would be long gone by now) he thought.
(By their trajectory they appeared to be moving toward the wormhole near Earth) Shoad thought.
Arap stood much shorter than Shoad and her body much smaller, but her mental acuity was just as sharp as she looked from one screen to another without typing in thoughts.
(Our records indicate Lin, his son, Pitta and Nesh, her daughter, were taking inoculations to enter Earth's atmosphere for a medium turn vacation) Arap thought.

THE MAN WHO DIDN'T WANT TO GO TO EARTH

(Follow that trajectory. Maybe we can head them off before they enter the wormhole) Tepa demanded with angst (I don't want anything to do with the rough man and don't want to be caught in his area causing mischief)

(He's dead) Arap turned back and looked at Tepa (He died on the way to Earth)

(His spirit still lives on in the people. Hurry, catch them before they move into rough man territory) Tepa thought.

Pa looked through his hidden adobe for certain items to take for the oncoming battle with Lin. He knew he didn't have much time, but when Shi's face appeared above his bed, he was startled.

(You are taking *too* long) Shi admitted (They probably arrived through the wormhole by now)

(No, protocol says they have a tiny turn, if they don't want to get sick on the travel) he eyed his wrist with red numbers (Be there shortly)

(Hurry) she blanked the screen.

When she turned about Tor stood in the background and they hissed in disapproval together.

Pa connected electron charges to his belt in case he needed to disarm a weapon and use that to his advantage. He wrapped the silver belt around his yellow robe and heard a silent alarm go off.

(Identify intruder) Pa thought to internal sensors.

(Sentry Authority) internal sensors responded in a male rough voice.

THE MAN WHO DIDN'T WANT TO GO TO EARTH

(That doesn't sound good. They must have picked up my signature through image motion. How long do we have before breach?) Pa asked.

(Now) the computer responded.

An explosion erupted about the green and yellow dome. Debris fell about the area as Pa's body disappeared in the smoke.

Within time sentries walked through what was left of the adobe. Their tall and silver bodies walked, bent-legged and ready with hands exposed for any return fire from the enemy. Tonie aimed her weapon and looked down, then sighed.

It was apparent Pa was dead with debris and bomb fragments in his face. His eyes looked half open as if he was watching an amazing sunset. His mouth parted as if he had words left unsaid.

(Who had set the yield?) she asked.

The sentries looked from one to another, almost confused. When Faro walked up and looked down and only shook his head negatively.

(I wanted him alive) Faro thought.

(I set the yield to minimum result for a breach) Sentry230 thought.

Faro suddenly shot Sentry230 in the chest and as he fell Tonie hissed in disapproval.

(He was our best explosive sentry) she thought.

(*It was*) Faro turned to Sentry232 (You oversee explosives. Remember to set the yield much lighter)

Sentry232 only nodded, then looked down at his former companion and wondered if *it* was next.

(What's our next move?) Tonie asked.

THE MAN WHO DIDN'T WANT TO GO TO EARTH

(Shi and Tor are nearby and should receive report of Pa's death on their signal patch. They will be on the run. We must watch the skies my sister, watch the skies) Faro thought.

(We can't wait for him) Shi thought as she gathered weaponry and placed them in her black air vehicle.
Tor followed her outside, as he eyed his wrist view screen.
(He has a valid reason, this time) Tor showed her his view screen.
Pa's face appeared on the view screen as deceased through an undetermined cause.
(Undetermined my ass. Can is on to us. We are out of here) she thought.
(They will be watching the skies for any departing ships) Tor thought.
(We will have to take our chances. We cannot stay here) Shi thought.

Ilic sat stunned when the face of Pa appeared above his view as deceased. When he hissed with disapproval and fear Char hurried from a back room in black robes with yellow edges, parted to show his chest and private parts.
(What is the problem? You found something?) Char asked.
(Yes, you, exposed) Ilic gestured down so that Char wrapped up quickly.
(Sorry a private session with my fifth companion on view screen) Char sat down and watched view screens (Where is the damning information?)

THE MAN WHO DIDN'T WANT TO GO TO EARTH

(The one about the fifth companion. Too much information) Ilic thought, disgusted.
Char only smiled slyly. Har walked in chewing a plant-based burger and wiped his face with a white cloth.
(Anxiety is way high in here. Found something we can use?) Har asked (Oh, let me see, the betrayer Pa is dead)
Char turned to Ilic.
(You should have led with that, Ilic) Char thought.
(It's all over the information feed. Don't need to read minds for that) Har thought.
(We really need to leave) Ilic thought (That's not far from our point)
(If they were on to us, we would be dead by now) Har thought (They will be checking the skies for departing ships. It may get ugly)
Ilic and Char stared at one another and nodded together.
(Let's take that chance) Ilic thought (I will need help locking down the cargo)
(I will give you all the help you will need) Har thought, determined to set Ilic's mind at ease.
(Don't need a flipping piece for this decision) Char thought as he flipped the thick object as it clumped in his hand with an odd sound and vibrated various colors.

12

I was stunned to see the face of Pa as it scrolled across deceased individuals within the last short turn. I suspected the betrayers (I am one of them) would end up dead, but to start seeing us on screens was a whole new deal.

I sat in a side room, with the lights dimmed and was startled to hear a voice and see a face! I almost jumped from my skin, but Pitta touched my shoulder for comfort.

(Are you trying to stop both my hearts?) I asked.

(Sorry. It would be too much of a loss for me to do that, because I care for you deeply; also, I have not the mental strength. We have two hearts, much easier to do that to a Human, who has one heart) she thought.

She stared at the screen and touched the small of my back that felt warm to the touch.

(Looks like the long arm of Can through his son, Faro) she thought.

(How do you know that?) I asked, alarmed.

She sat next to me and began moving her fingers on barely seen numbers and letters. Her green and yellow robe brushed against my leg, but I tried to ignore it as we focused on the view screens.

(I can do this mentally, but I am not up to it. See, Faro, Tepa, and their sister Tonie. Tepa broke off and is looking for me *specifically*) she thought.

(Why you *specifically*?) I asked.

(Certain finger strokes have pointed electronic eyes in my direction and I have hidden security that watch out for that. I believe that Can

THE MAN WHO DIDN'T WANT TO GO TO EARTH

wants me as his sex slave, but his son, Tepa is not having it) she thought.
    I sat, amazed as she moved in and out of visuals, numbers and letters.
    (Tepa is either protective for your good or his good) I thought.
    (His good. He wants me all to himself) she thought (But they will both be disappointed, because I will be heading to Earth in how long...?)
    (One tiny turn) I admitted.

    Nesh noticed several ships moving at quick speed before I saw them. We had just started the countdown to move into the wormhole for Earth. Our lips moved with mental thought and synchronicity when an audio interrupted our levity and hope.
    (Earthbound vessel, please desist all functions and open to receive boarding from the Authority of Great Leader Can) a robot's audio commenced.
    I leaned forward in a silver chair and gripped the chair's arms tightly. Nesh and Hut, who sat before me in separate silver chairs looked back, terrified. Pitta who sat to my right, stood, alarmed.
    (We cannot let them board) Pitta thought.
    (I have no intention of letting them) I thought to the computer's command (Move us out of here, slowly, to the shade)

    The shade was an anomaly in space that was able to shut out much of the light from our sun and many electronics after a medium turn. It acted as a mist in space. The mystery of its existence had never been solved, but it showed that there were

THE MAN WHO DIDN'T WANT TO GO TO EARTH

even areas in space where even we could not go without horror.

(The shade, father?) Hut asked.

(Many went into the shade never to return) Nesh warned.

(I know. It's either that or them) I thought.

We coasted for some time as the shade quickly engulfed our ship. It acted as something that masked light, but in time allowed the Central Sun to push through in various spots.

It was a vast area and only ended at the beginning of Pro Planet or Pro as we called it and ended on the edge of Harlo1 or the Harmonics first planet before the other three came into view.

Ships lost, coasted in the shade, its crew most likely mummified after many long terms.

(This is not good) Hut stood and leaned on a nearby chair, eyes wide.

(I'm scared) Nesh ran to her mother for support and a comforting hug.

(I'm surprised they haven't fired on us, yet) I thought.

(I believe they want to take us alive) Pitta thought.

(That's to our advantage) I thought.

(Not for me) Pitta thought with eyes downcast.

(Me neither) I nodded.

Hut, filled with anxiety, looked in the rearview of the ship.

(I don't see them following) Hut noticed.

(They are probably debating on whether to enter the shade) I thought.

THE MAN WHO DIDN'T WANT TO GO TO EARTH

(We can use that to our advantage) Pitta thought.

13

(Don't let them get away) Tepa thought to his Commander1 robot.

Commander1 was a tall robot of dark and gray colors with green eyes and a metallic voice. Many had found his voice in their head to be unnerving and blocked his voice with audio only commands.

"Looks like they are heading for the shade. We may lose them. We can disable their engines with one blast) Commander1 said as his dark hand hovered over a red button.

(Don't you dare touch that button) Tepa thought (We may accidentally destroy the ship; then where would we be? Father would be furious. He wants Pitta alive, follow them into the shade and try to outmaneuver them) Tepa thought with angst, because deep down he did not want his prize destroyed.

(Slow speed to the shade) Commander1 informed the robot crew who sat in various spots in green chairs.

(Entering the shade will cause disorientation after a small turn among the crew and ship. One long turn and we will be all deceased) Tepa thought, worried (Let's get in and out quickly)

"Going in," Commander1 said with a metallic, unnerving voice.

Tonie, who eyed all search points noticed Tepa's ship vanish off the screen. She immediately notified Faro through the view screen.

THE MAN WHO DIDN'T WANT TO GO TO EARTH

(Just lost Tepa's ship through the shade. How long should we give him before we send a search and find?) she asked.

Faro looked irritated and hissed.

(Maybe one short turn. We must get to them before their ship breaks down and is nonfunctional. This is a distraction. I have enough to do with finding the betrayers let alone one woman for the purpose of lust. Despicable) he growled.

(To capture Lin's ship will yield one betrayer and a trophy for father. It's worth the pursuit) she admitted.

(We can agree to disagree. Let's focus for the time on Shi and Tor, where are they?) he asked.

(We have narrowed down the search to the Longmont Mountains in Jan, we have points closing in) she thought.

Shi and Tor maneuvered slowly through several points above Jan in a black and yellow ship, before they were able to move at quick speed.

With their ship in stealth, they were almost invisible, but any loud noise from within could focus instruments externally.

So, they barely breathed and hovered and coasted so as not to strike space debris, which were plentiful before the atmospheric burnup.

(I think we are safe for now) Shi thought.

(I see no pursuit in progress) Tor looked in the rearview.

(Let's go to Pro) she thought.

(Pro it is) he thought.

THE MAN WHO DIDN'T WANT TO GO TO EARTH

Faro looked intensely at his wide view screen that appeared almost like jelly underwater and hissed with disapproval several times. When Tonie's face appeared, he cursed mentally and through thin lips.

(We just missed them. I don't see how they got past our air security accept through stealth) he thought.

(With stealth it will be most difficult to track them and as time goes on almost impossible) she thought.

(You focus on them, *only*. I will prepare a force to follow brother before he gets trapped in the shade) Faro's image dissolved in blackness.

(Somebody's not happy) she thought to herself.

Har stared up at the sky from their point which extended from the room as a flat roof and buffer points that were electronic in case of falls. He noticed several ships moving in certain patterns and figured they were still searching.

(They lost them) Har thought.
(How do you know?) Ilic asked.
(With some audio chatter on my voice finder, some still use the dead language, rarely used, I detect much frustration, disappointment) Har turned to Ilic and pointed (We can make a point of escape with cargo, right through there, before dark fall)

Char walked into the open upper area and looked up. He was impressed with Har's ability to surmise certain points and come to clear conclusions.

THE MAN WHO DIDN'T WANT TO GO TO EARTH

(We have one small turn before dark fall) Char thought.
(Let's leave now) Har thought.

THE MAN WHO DIDN'T WANT TO GO TO EARTH

14

My hands remained gripped to the silver chair as we maneuvered through shaded areas that began to open to space, stars and planets. We moved the ship well above the orbit of Shun, sometimes called Harlo1 or the first planet moving into the Harmonic Realm.

Shun (Harlo1) was lifeless due to the last destroyer war. Giant spider creatures tried to terraform the planet, but rough man Mars and those from Phaes obliterated many of the destroyers through planet killers and balls of light that turned to destroy ships.

We all peered at the destruction that looked like dark colors meshed with gases. Debris, still trapped from the war moved as if alive.

(We will be okay if we don't get pulled in its orbit) I thought.

(How long do you want to wait here?) Hut asked, terrified.

(One medium turn should do it) I turned to Pitta who agreed with a nod.

(We are outside the shade, so we are safe from complete ship degradation. We have some repairs to make before we move forward) I thought.

Nesh, petrified, ran into her back bedroom. Hut followed to comfort her.

(Oh, how I miss the rough man now) I thought.

(His spirit is in all of us) Pitta thought somberly.

I, surprised by this response, turned to her with eyebrows raised, then turned to the expanse and watched the debris swirl as if alive.

THE MAN WHO DIDN'T WANT TO GO TO EARTH

(I do not see them) Tepa looked left and right.
"They could not have gone far. The shade will not allow quick speed, unless their ship would have completely failed by now. They are close," Commander1 said.
(Then find them) Tepa thought sternly.

Faro approached the shade and hesitated with a fleet of ships. He knew moving into the gray matter could cause multiple ship failures. He walked in a circle with his head down, not sure what to do, until Great Leader Can, his father viewscreened him.
(Report) Can ordered (No need I can see you are walking in circles, just like you did as a child whenever you had to make a hard decision)
(If we go in the shade, it could be bad, father. I am weighing the factors. I just need a moment to think) Faro admitted.
(An effective leader takes control of the situation and damned time to think. Your brother could be dying in there. What are you going to do?) Can asked.
Faro pressed his pink fist against his red mouth and made sounds of angst, until he grunted and decided to do it for his brother.
(Now, that is a good leader) Can thought (Notify me shortly of your progress)
When Can blackened the screen Faro decided not to enter the shade but knew his father would punish his indecision with degrading words and assignments to various planets for menial purposes.

THE MAN WHO DIDN'T WANT TO GO TO EARTH

(Enter the shade) Faro demanded.
As the ship slowly became engulfed by the destructive mist, Faro closed his eyes as if to block out his most recent decision.

(We have been here long enough) I thought.
Hut smiled as he sat below me and began to touch buttons.
(Where to?) Hut asked.
I hesitated to give instructions, because I was concerned an emergency could commence where Hut, not experienced, would not know how to handle, but I quickly pressed down any worries and Hut, seeing my struggle, smiled.
(We will need to take the long way around the wormhole. Let's take the scenic route, no rush) I thought.
Pitta seemed pleased by my decision and rarely gave a response or thought to my decisions. I sensed she wanted to see how I reacted under pressure.
When it came to Urbanite relationships this was a way for females to select males for companionship on the way they reacted under pressure.
I knew she originated on Pro, but their ways were similar when it came to selecting mates.
I really did not see myself as in her league per male companionship, but she had been giving me strong signals by "crashing the party," hand holding and gentle kisses, all encouraged by her.
I thought it was a test of my stern ability to stay focused and if I gave in to her wiles I would end up on the floor, upside down, with a possible broken limb.

THE MAN WHO DIDN'T WANT TO GO TO EARTH

As we coasted away at slow speed I stood near the controls, just in case we encountered an emergency, but my son became defensive and eyed me.
(Father, really? I do know what I am doing) Hut thought (I have ship flight training)
(I know that, but you never know your reaction in an emergency) I thought.
Hut stared, disappointed, with mouth downturned. I raised my hands as a sign of surrender, as Hut turned around and began to chart a course forward.

(I see nothing in the shade) Tepa thought angrily (They must have moved beyond, but where?)
"Cannot track ships in the shade, Subleader," Commander1 admitted.
(I know that) Tepa thought, irritated (Let's leave through the Harmonic Realms, backtrack, go around a quick speed and head them off at the wormhole. If they are not already there)
"Our ships are trashed," Commander1 admitted.
(What?) Tepa looked alarmed.
"The instruments tell it all," Commander1 pointed with a dark hand. "We traveled too fast. We need to pause our roll and do maintenance on the engines. Look, let's wait at Shun."
Tepa sighed and gripped his sides with thin, pink hands.
(I found remnants of another ship in this area) sentry211 thought as it leaned forward.

THE MAN WHO DIDN'T WANT TO GO TO EARTH

(Move it to time stamp visual) Tepa thought, excited.

A ship came into view with dark coloring and light that reflected from the central sun. Then it was gone.

(They did not stay long, maybe a medium turn. Slow speed to Planet Dun, then the visuals dissolve) sentry211 admitted.

(Dun is uninhabited due to the destroyer war, so they won't be hiding there) Tepa wondered (We need two ships to follow them so we can engage without incident, is our entire fleet trashed?)

"For one small turn only one ship is able to make the pursuit," Commander1 said.

(Take me to that ship and remind me to change your voice box. It irritates me) Tepa thought.

Commander1 stared, confused, as if a train barreled at top speed, with signals blaring, and it was nothing he could do to stop it.

THE MAN WHO DIDN'T WANT TO GO TO EARTH

15

(There is one ship approaching) Pitta admitted to me as I showered in the back room (Begin elusive maneuvers. I will be there shortly)

I slid on quick clothes of green robes wrapped in blue ties and black boots with green ties. I combed my hair back and rinsed my mouth with blue good smelling dye that whitened the teeth.

Nesh and Hut sat in forward chairs and stared at the expanse filled with debris of Du, which looked like Shun, but filled more with a red substance that looked like blood.

Nesh immediately left the room and Hut struggled to not follow, but he was more intrigued than frightened and sat, riveted.

When I sat in the chair, I was refreshed but filled with angst. Pitta gave me a weak smile.

(I should get so clean) she thought.

(You can when we are out of danger) I looked in the rearview (It's one ship)

(They should bypass us. I am under Planet Dun's orbit. I don't think they detected us, yet) she thought.

(We will find out momentarily) I thought as the ship moved closer.

(It's a scout ship, probably sent to find us through a time stamp visual) she thought.

As the ship approached it was twice the size of our ship and caused trepidation among us as it slowed.

(I thought they would be in this area. At slow speed they would arrive here) Tepa thought.

THE MAN WHO DIDN'T WANT TO GO TO EARTH

Sentry222 had a silver and black look with robes that were wrapped around his thin frame. He had green eyes that scanned and searched for enemy craft.

(They were here for a tiny turn) Sentry 222 admitted.

(Project time stamp visuals) Tepa thought.

(Too close to the planet. Cannot detect because of distortion. We will have to move back some length) Sentry222 thought.

(Do it) Tepa ordered.

(They are retreating) Hut thought, relieved.

(No, it's a trick. Let's keep this orbit below the planet for now) I thought.

I turned to Pitta for confirmation and nodded as she smiled with my skepticism.

(By this visual it appears they moved with Dun's orbit) Sentry222 admitted as the ship visual showed a weak facsimile of a time before.

(Follow that trajectory around the planet) Tepa demanded.

Sentry3, built with red eyes and a silver and black body remained quiet in thought. It began to have angst, built into its system to bring tension and Urb-like qualities for better decisions.

(We will have to be aware of the gravitational pull. The planet is unbalanced from the previous war) Sentry3 thought.

(I'm aware of that) Tepa thought.

(They are moving in synchronicity to our orbit. They should be on top of us in a tiny turn) Hut thought as fear filled his frame.

THE MAN WHO DIDN'T WANT TO GO TO EARTH

I raised my hand to calm his emotions which were all over the place.

(We can make a run for it at quick speed) Pitta thought.

(It may not be enough. It's a scout ship able to move faster than the average ship, which is what we have. We need to surprise them. Something to set them off balance) I sighed and touched some buttons (Ship, arm cannon one and fire on my go)

Hut stood suddenly.

(You had that cannon put in, father? I thought you didn't have time) Hut thought.

I tried to hold my grin and forced a snarl instead, because it was not in my heart to do this.

(You placed a cannon in?) Pitta asked (How did I miss that?)

(You can't see everything, Pitta. Only God sees all) I thought (Ship, arm cannon two)

(Father, two cannons?) he remained standing, completely surprised.

(Two cannons armed and ready to fire) the ship thought.

When the massive scout ship appeared suddenly above them, ominous, Tepa's image appeared on their view screen as well. He smiled; triumphant he had found them.

(Prepare to be boarded) Tepa thought.

(Ship, fire) I thought.

Two cannons erupted and traveled to their ship as massive fireballs. Tepa's face vanished and I sat in morbid thoughts on another life possibly taken.

Tepa fell to the side as the two bursts erupted into his ship. Unprepared the ship began

THE MAN WHO DIDN'T WANT TO GO TO EARTH

to spiral out of control as Sentry222 and Sentry3 tried to keep control.

(We need to stay above orbit, or we will be lost in Dun) Sentry3 thought.

Tepa pulled himself up and touched some buttons to steady the damaged ship, but as the ship began to balance it moved into the planet's orbit and they struggled not be pulled completely into its black and red mass.

(I cannot do it) I thought (I don't want more blood on my hands. Ship, ways to extricate enemy ship from orbit)

There was a slight pause as I awaited information. Then, Pitta was at my side.

(If we are not pulled down with them) Pitta thought.

(Cannon eruptions around the ship's frame can cause it to regain its balance from energy and fire. I can initiate action, or you can initiate) the ship thought.

(Initiate action ship) I thought and turned to Pitta (I don't think my eyes are that good)

She smiled weakly and squeezed my shoulder with a strong hand.

Cannon fire erupted around the ship as it appeared to go deeper into the orbit. Then, it vanished, and I assumed lost; but within a tiny turn it emerged with burns, damaged, but not totally gone.

I sighed, relieved.

(Ship, quick speed to Baud) I thought.

(Quick speed) the ship complied.

THE MAN WHO DIDN'T WANT TO GO TO EARTH

(He tried to finish us off, but he only helped us) Tepa coughed in the smoke (Can we pursue?)

Sentry3 disagreed with a negative shake of his silver and black head.

(We are trashed) Sentry3 thought.

(He was not trying to destroy us, but to keep us off his tail. The final cannon attack was to help us climb from the abyss. It was precisely placed to help us use the energy projection to our advantage. Still want to pursue after we are able?) Sentry222 asked.

Tepa could only look and not make a final decision. He sighed and looked down, defeated, for now.

16

(We need to rest. The next planet is Baud, uninhabitable like Dun and Shun. We can park far above its orbit and take a break) I thought to the others.

(There is always Planet Tab. It's habitable) Pitta thought, anguished.

(Tab is not habitable to us, unless you want to be absorbed. They will need to implement environmental systems so we can breathe) I thought.

Hut shook his head from side to side.

(I don't want to be absorbed) he turned to Nesh (Do you want to be absorbed?)

She pressed her thin lips together and repeated his head movements. It was clear she was going through a great amount of stress and fear. It was obvious that Pitta noticed this but was weighing her options before making a final decision.

I watched Pitta and she stared at me with determined eyes. I parked the ship above Baud's dark planet of browns and blues mixed with red. It terrified Nesh and battled to stay in her seat, so as not to run in the back room through fear.

(Why don't you guys watch the skies for us?) I asked.

Hut nodded with Nesh, and Pitta and I hurried into our back room, sealed the door and stared at each other in angst.

(You want out?) I asked.

(It has crossed my mind. Nesh is taking this in and she is not handling it well) Pitta thought.

THE MAN WHO DIDN'T WANT TO GO TO EARTH

(We need to park and service our engines soon, a slow turn after Tab and we should be at Pro, far from the wormhole and the Authoritarians) I thought.

(Sounds like a plan) she thought, but her eyes misted over with disappointment (I am sorry for bailing on you)

I hugged her to comfort.

(You are not bailing. You are sacrificing for your daughter. Let's tell them the news)

Nesh and Hut bowed their heads in disappointment and remained silent as we coasted past Planet Tab with its beautiful colors of blue, green and gold.

Faro's team struggled to stay in the shade for long as possible but extricated their ships at the same spot they entered. Faro sighed as he stared at his instruments and wondered where Tepa extricated.

A blue and green tall robot stared platonically with silver eyes. It was Commander4 and Faro found it useless at times, but when it moved forward on long legs it gave vital information.

(Your brother is safe and is taking a short turn around the shade and should be here shortly) Commander4 admitted with a dry smile.

(Finally, some good news) Faro smiled weakly.

(The betrayer Lin and Pitta are not captured) Commander4 thought.

(Can we pursue?) Faro asked.

THE MAN WHO DIDN'T WANT TO GO TO EARTH

(They are taking a long turn around Tab according to my scans. We are not functional to pursue now. We will need a medium turn before our engines can be activated for full throttle) Commander4 thought.

(Medium turn we should be able to pursue after their long turn) Faro thought.

(It's possible) Commander4 thought but remained unsure.

(Why do you have doubts?) Faro asked.

(Something is not right about the whole pursuit. My circuits are not meshed about it) Commander4 thought.

(You are fitted with circuits that sense uneven circumstances to make better choices. I will consider that) Faro thought, unnerved.

Shi was stressed as they entered Pro's atmosphere. She suspected an ambush as soon as they cleared the pressures of planet entry, but after moving below where vast waters and small strips of land mass came into view, Shi's stress lessened.

(I guess we are not all that important) Shi thought.

(I don't want to be all that important. We are above the Stay Place, going in) Tor, turned his head in a silver helmet as electronics appeared above his head.

(Be careful of the Stay Place. Could be a trap too) Shi thought.

Tor only nodded his head and leveled the ship to spread its wings as debris cascaded out and they settled down in an open field of various ships.

The Stay Place (Hotel) was a large adobe of blue, white and green colors that welcomed guests who had special monies that resembled bulky coins of various colors.

Some coins gave off certain perky sounds when handled and there had been many guests who sat in long chairs, stared out of windows and watched their coins, mesmerized.

(We will carry our own bags) Shi projected thought to a short black and green robot.

(Besides I think our bags may be a bit heavy for your taste) Tor smiled mischievously.

Shi carried two large bags and Tor carried three. The short robot only stared with bent eyebrows, surprised, as it floated away to help other new arrivals.

(We are on the upper level, able to get away with air pockets on our boots. Our air vehicle is right below us and can be received quickly, just in case) Shi thought.

(All points covered) Tor thought as he smiled at passing visitors (Pretty busy tonight)

(Let's get out of this traffic of bodies then we can lay low and go from there) Shi thought.

When we arrived at the Stay Place Near the Strip Lands, I did not suspect any trouble. I believed the betrayers who survived my explosion were long gone and the Authoritarians were held near the wormhole to stop us from coming through, which we had no intentions of doing, thanks to them.

I looked at my green wrist timer and looked back at the declining sun's rays. Pitta walked close to me, leery of Authoritarian Agents that posed as objects like suitcases and vending machines.

THE MAN WHO DIDN'T WANT TO GO TO EARTH

I thought I saw Shi and Tor and froze in my tracks so that Hut and Nesh crashed into my backside.
(What is it, father?) Hut asked.
(You see something?) Pitta asked, as her body tensed for battle.
(No) I raised my hand to steady everyone (I thought I saw Shi and Tor, but it couldn't be them) I sighed and patted Nesh and Hut on the shoulders (Let's get some rest)

(I need to scope out things) Tor thought as he adjusted dark glasses on his face as they wrapped around his nose and ears.
(You look too obvious) Shi thought.
(What does *too obvious* mean?) Tor asked.
(Other words you look *silly*) Shi thought (We should both be laying low)
(Just a sweep of the place, just in case) Tor thought (Plus, I am hungry. Want something?)
She shook her head negatively and sat on the bed and stared at a declining sun.
(I will bring you a rejuvenating blend of a green and brown drink, your favorite) Tor thought.
(Just as well) she thought.
Wrapped in green and black robes, black boots with sunglasses and a wicked smile, Tor emerged from the room and gave his best face to those who passed.

(We need to order in) I thought (Pitta, Hut and Nesh, let me know what you want and…)
(I need to case the place) Pitta thought, filled with anxiety.

THE MAN WHO DIDN'T WANT TO GO TO EARTH

(You know you could expose us to the Authoritarians. You should stay with us until morning, so we can hatch a plan to leave) I thought.
(Then what? Keep running? Is that your plan?) she asked as her angst rose.
I felt confrontation as it oozed from her, but I did not bite. I held my thoughts as Nesh calmed her with a gentle rub on the hand.
(Mother, could you stay with us and not leave?) Nesh asked.
Pitta only touched her daughter's face and smiled to comfort her concerns.
(I will not be long) Pitta thought.

17

Over five hundred long turns ago, with too many hazardous aftereffects to the individuals' mind and body, many planets in the Jan Region banned the use of shifting technology and developed a vacuum tube from ship to ship.

(What happened with the pursuit of Lin and his entourage?) Faro asked Tepa through the view screen.

Faro sensed that Tepa was too embarrassed to expose his experience through view screen and he remained silent until he slid in a tube that connected to each ship and was projected through energetic pull.

As the tube slid open Tepa felt slightly dizzy but retained his balance and followed his brother to a far back room without cameras and microphones.

(He saved my life) Tepa thought (He fired cannons at me, and we were not ready, but he projected more cannon fire, and we lifted out of the abyss of gravity on Dun)

Faro sighed and looked down and about, not sure what to make of it.

(Soon father will want a report. What will we say?) Tepa asked.

(The truth. He scans faster than any machine. I still want to pursue it but do not destroy the ship. I want to save his prize possession and ask why you were saved?) Faro asked.

Tepa stared at him intently.

(You are thinking about giving them a reprieve?) Tepa asked, surprised.

(Not in the presence of father. We must keep this hidden. Even Commander4 cannot connect the dots when it comes to this chase) Faro thought.

(Commander4 is fitted with ethical routines to make better decisions when it comes to battle) Tepa thought.

(You know what father will do with her when he gets her) Faro thought (But, you have no intention of giving her to him. You want her for yourself)

(The moment he connects with a view screen he will know all that we thought of. Our careers will be over. We may be in prison for life) Tepa thought.

(Disable the view screens, Ship Connections) Faro commanded.

(*Ship connections have been disabled*) an internal voice thought.

(That will only hold him for a moment) Tepa thought (We need something long term)

(Pursuit will commence shortly. If we can apprehend them before the Authoritarians come in it might turn out to our favor. We can be the heroes for a change) Faro thought.

(We are coming upon the Earth wormhole by this location) Char thought as he moved his hands around to position the ship (We are far enough back to view the Authoritarians, but not so close to move into the wormhole and elude them)

(They are not looking for *us*) Har thought and turned to Ilic who sat across from him (They are looking for *him*)

THE MAN WHO DIDN'T WANT TO GO TO EARTH

Ilic felt uncomfortable as Har glared at him like a tasty meal, but what Ilic felt was betrayal. He knew then Har wanted to throw him to the wolves.

(We should turn around until we can think of a plan) Ilic thought as he moved to the edge of his seat.

(What is the use of coming all the way out here...) Char thought.

(We should turn around) Ilic thought with angst.

Char turned to Har for confirmation who nodded his head. Char moved his hands as the ship coasted backward and away.

(That was pointless) Char thought.

(I need time to think) Ilic thought as he wrung his hands together and stood to walk around.

Geta was 104 long turns old, still young by Urbanite standards. He wore gray and yellow robes that were wrapped tightly over his six-foot frame.

He had a crew of five robotic Authoritarians who used connections to find information on the true whereabouts of his former partner Ilic.

(I am coming for you partner) Geta thought with a wicked smile as his black and yellow ship moved effortlessly through constellations to find its target.

Pitta purchased a large hat with dark sunglasses that were wrapped around her face. She knew it was an eye-catching disguise; but knew it would block any face recognition software for a limited time.

THE MAN WHO DIDN'T WANT TO GO TO EARTH

She had her back turned and looked down at the hat as she adjusted it with her hands, when a man almost collided with her. She briefly looked up when he excused himself.

When she looked down, she knew her cover was blown. It was Tor and he appeared to have recognized her; but he pretended he had not.

When he threw a jagged blade at her, she side stepped so that it killed a male vendor through the forehead. As the elderly Pro alien fell forward his cart crashed down and items spilled everywhere. Screams came from various places as Tor and Pitta began hand to hand combat.

She whipped around with long legs and connected with his jaw so that he fell back onto other vendors' cart and more screams filled the atmosphere.

Authoritarians, hidden, began to change from luggage, vending machines and push carts to stand several feet tall and aimed their weapons through hands.

Laser fire exploded everywhere as Tor and Pitta hurried away as aliens, petrified, pulled their loved ones to a nearby safety wall.

Pitta, in deep fear and enraged he had exposed them, began to pummel Tor who tried to stop the blows from the floor.

(You are a dumb ass) she thought.

(Not as dumb as you) Tor thought and flipped her above his head.

When laser fire exploded about their bodies they scattered in different directions. Tor ran behind a tall wall while Pitta hurried down moving electronic stairs.

THE MAN WHO DIDN'T WANT TO GO TO EARTH

Geta smiled as he honed on his former partner's ship through stealth. With certain movements and vibrations his ship appeared invisible, but as it approached from behind Har noticed a glitch on his screen.
(We are being shadowed) Har thought.
Ilic's heart skipped a beat as he stopped pacing to peer at his screen. Char, who flipped his thick coin began to prepare the ship to run.
(Who is it?) Char asked.
(I don't know) Har thought.
Suddenly, Geta, enraged, fired on them as their ship spun almost out of control. Har growled and tried to gain balance.
(Prepare cannons and return fire) Har thought.
(I don't know who we are firing at. They are using stealth) Char thought.
Char tried to return fire, but the cannon only shot in blackened space.
(One hit will expose them, but we cannot stay here. Move out and try to gain balance) Har commanded.
(Getting the hell out of here) Char thought.
Geta demanded to follow them and keep firing to offset balance.
(I don't want them destroyed. I want to bring them to the Authoritarians for a nice price) Geta thought.

THE MAN WHO DIDN'T WANT TO GO TO EARTH

18

Pitta ran at top speed as four tall robotic Authoritarians pursued along the walls and the ceiling. She connected to Lin through the view screen.

(Get out. We are compromised) she thought.

(Damn) Lin thought.

Pitta disconnected the line and flipped backwards as the laser struck the floor. She flipped on the back of one Authoritarian and severed its head with a short sheath.

When it fell forward, she jumped on the back of another and severed its head in the same way.

The remaining two looked shoulder to shoulder, in case she used their shoulders for support; but she used this time to jump below and head out the door with several other visitors.

When she noticed Nesh, Hut and Lin her smile was wide. Satisfied, they were near safe for the time she turned a nearby corner and two robotic Authoritarians pursued.

I know I could not leave her without doing something. Nesh screamed anguish in my ear while throwing unintelligible thoughts. I asked Hut to calm her a little while I thought and raised the ship.

Hut tried to calm Nesh down as I turned the ship on its balance, eyed the Authoritarians, and fired one cannon.

As the projectile exploded into the ground, I then knew it was not a very good idea, because Pitta could no longer be seen.

THE MAN WHO DIDN'T WANT TO GO TO EARTH

I hovered through the smoke and debris until I saw movement and trusted it was her as Nesh and Hut yelled in horror!

It was her. The plan barely worked as she approached, dirty, scraped and the robots were eliminated. I slid open the door and we helped her get on and took off into a dark sky.

(We need to leave, *now*) Tor thought as he arrived in the room with Shi.

At full rest Shi leaped through the air and began to slide bags on her back. She cursed mentally and through pursed red lips amid white teeth.

(I thought I heard explosions, but I attributed it to construction. I told you not to go out there) She thought.

(It was the rough man girl, Pitta. She recognized me. I had to do something) he thought.

(What did you do?) Shi asked.

(Had my ass handed to me like she did the rough man. I believe that rumor was true) he thought as he grabbed the remaining bags.

(If she was here that means…) she paused in thought.

(So was Lin) he finished her thought.

(We will have to be careful. More Authoritarians are surely on the way) he thought.

She peered up and down the hallway and motioned for him to follow.

Geta growled as the larger ship eluded him through a gaseous constellation like the shade, but not as destructive on ship instruments.

THE MAN WHO DIDN'T WANT TO GO TO EARTH

Named *Shoran's Way* it consisted of gases from various stars and debris from stars that collapsed.

In the past many bandits hid their ships and played chase and hide until the Authoritarians exhausted their energy and were forced to return to base on Urb and recharge.

(I don't see them) Char leaned forward and flipped his thick object of luck.

(Our balance was near collapse. If he had disabled our balance, we would have been ripe for boarding) Har thought grimly.

(He stayed away from our engines. It doesn't appear like he was trying to destroy us) Ilic thought.

(No) Har turned to Ilic (He didn't want to damage the cargo)

(Cargo check) Char stood quickly and walked only a few steps to the back. He returned with a smile (Cargo safe)

(We may have to charge the wormhole to get through) Har thought (Let's do a system-wide check and repair)

Ilic trembled as he thought of charging the wormhole with so many ships ready to return fire. Har knew Ilic had deep doubts about the whole plan.

(We have the element of surprise) Har thought.

Ilic nodded but didn't think the element of surprise was enough.

I really didn't want to go to Earth now, but it appeared as the safest place, suddenly. As we hovered above the atmosphere I contemplated

THE MAN WHO DIDN'T WANT TO GO TO EARTH

going to Jan, again, but this time on the other side of the planet.

(Jan seems like a good idea) Pitta thought.
(We are running out of options) I thought.

Hut sat with Nesh and watched the area for Authoritarians. I positioned the ship for Jan as we coasted at medium speed and hoped for the best.

THE MAN WHO DIDN'T WANT TO GO TO EARTH

19

Great Can sat as if immobile in his long-backed chair in the HQ of Planet Urb. With its several hubs that connected to other distribution centers, it was filled with constant activity.

Except in his office, which were filled with former great leaders and electronic pictures that shifted in and out of focus.

He sat as if in daze, until the signal beeped almost silent. He faintly smiled and touched a button.

(Report, Laird) Can replied.

Laird was a small robot developed for information research and nothing else. This gave it much quicker access through information blocks (firewalls), more than other robots had.

Laird also acted as an aid and advisor to Can and his immediate staff. It had gold-plated squares positioned on its skin that shimmered from various hues of gold.

(Your sons have disconnected the ship from external stimuli. The audio is inoperable without the view monitors. Ingenious way to hide something) Laid admitted.

(They tried that same thing over fifty long rotations ago when they were stealing from my private till. Did not work then and it will not work now. The result was imprisonment, at least forty-long rotations, until their loyal mother persuaded me to release them on eternal probation) Can thought.

(Incoming call from the loyal mother) Laird thought.

THE MAN WHO DIDN'T WANT TO GO TO EARTH

I was on the edge of my seat as we approached Jan. Jan did sustain some decimation from Phaes' eruption. They also received various Phasees and rejected any housing for Fumans. This left the Fumans with almost nowhere to go, but Urb; Pro did not receive any Fumans.

Jan had a population of nearly 5 billion Janeites and had long constructs of towers and large bodies of water.

Much of the population resided on its shorelines as water vehicles carried bodies to various spots. With small islands that connected to various points, this was where nearly 14000 Phasees were allowed to live, with constraints.

With nominal damage from Phaes' destruction, top leader Bal, 732 long years old, remained angered by the damage, but many close constituents encouraged him not to make matters worse by going after the Fumans.

They encouraged him to let the Urb leader handle the Fumans, thus keeping his hands clean.

This was the area that I landed, because of some tolerance of our position. I felt the Phasees would understand, and they welcomed us with open arms and a bright blue and yellow tower that was many looks up.

(I don't know if I like this idea) Hut thought.

(We have no other choice but to remain running. The hidden hills are compromised. Soon we will run out of ship energy. We must recharge and rest) I thought.

(What is with the height?) Nesh asked.

(Janeites like their heights) I thought in jest.

THE MAN WHO DIDN'T WANT TO GO TO EARTH

Two elevators resided one at the top and another on the ground. As we took the elevator up the other elevator descended so that an elevator almost remained on the ground.

I didn't find this very secure because I thought if someone wanted to catch us, they only had to take an elevator up.

(They have a locking security that will not let them into our adobe unless requested) Pitta thought as she read my concerns (They would be literally trapped in the air until we allowed them in)

(That would only work if we saw them coming) I thought.

She agreed with a shrug of her shoulders.

We took a well-lit elevator to its top where it opened to a brightly lit area of rooms and viewscreens. Robots, formerly immobile, moved about to take our baggage and to fix meals.

We stared at each other, not sure how to take the hospitality, until Pitta headed for the shower.

(I'm first) she demanded.

I smiled and we all began to settle into our rooms. Nesh was afraid to sleep alone, due to past violent confrontations, dead planets, and weird, out of this world dreams, brought on by chemical applications to travel.

I had to admit the dreams of creatures with two heads stomping around to devour and crashing ships did not seem prophetic, but it all unnerved us just the same.

Pitta and I agreed she could sleep in the same room where Hut stayed, if he did not mind. He was more surprised we agreed to the setup, but

THE MAN WHO DIDN'T WANT TO GO TO EARTH

I pushed Nesh's short bed on electronic balancers so that it floated without trouble.

With beds separated by a small table and a lamp, Pitta and I stood in the doorway and eyed them as the lights dimmed until only a nightlight remained on the floor.

(Just like brother and sister) I thought.

I touched a button and a gray electronic shade moved across to give them sleeping privacy. I walked into a nearby area of the room, where Pitta hovered, unsure of something.

(What?) I asked.

(I know I cannot be around all the time for my daughter) she started.

I nodded (No one can be around all the time, only God is all)

She only nodded and looked down with tears in her eyes.

(What is bothering you? I cannot read you with the blocking techniques) I admitted.

(If something was to happen to me) she started, and pressed her thin tan lips together (I want you to take over the watchful eye of her protection)

I only nodded and touched her shoulder.

(I am honored to be like a parent to your daughter if you will do the same for my son) I thought.

She suddenly hugged me tightly. I reciprocated and we stayed this way for some time.

THE MAN WHO DIDN'T WANT TO GO TO EARTH

THE OBSESSION

THE MAN WHO DIDN'T WANT TO GO TO EARTH

HENRY DAVID THOREAU QUOTE
"What is the use of a house if you haven't got a tolerable planet to put it on?"
FAMILIAR LETTERS

THE MAN WHO DIDN'T WANT TO GO TO EARTH

20

Dorr, Great Can's Upper Companion, or first partner looked with light features, green lips and black paintings across her face. It was a look of distinguishment which she reveled in.

(You look amazing, dear) Can smiled.

(Don't try to butter me up, Can. What about our sons? What have you heard?) she asked.

(Nothing yet. They have disconnected their ship lines. I am sending an Amada to find out what is going on. You know the last time this happened they ended up in prison for a long time) Can thought.

(Oh, this was a bad idea to give them responsibility. You should never have given them those positions. Sometimes I think you do things like this to see them fail and revel in their failure) she thought, angry.

(No, I am trying to teach them to be responsible leaders. I am training them to take this chair from me when the time is right) he thought.

(Leadership is not for everyone) she thought.

(So right you are) he looked at a view screen (The Amada should be there by now. I will send you an update as things transpire)

(You do that, and if anything was to happen to my sons, I would never forgive you) she thought.

(*Our sons*) he emphasized (You never asked about our daughter, Tonie)

(Oh, she can take care of herself) she thought (I trained her myself)

THE MAN WHO DIDN'T WANT TO GO TO EARTH

(Oh) he thought about her words and blanked the screen as a new realization came to him.

(Daughter, daughter) Great Can thought through view screen to Tonie.

Tonie was surprised to receive a call from her father this late in the evening. She knew he rested early and rose late after the sun's rising.

(My brothers failed you, father) she surmised from her long-backed black chair (You want me to find your obsession, your trophy)

(She is not a trophy, daughter) he squinted from the word (I just need for her to *comply*)

(She will never *comply*, father and this angers you. You never forced mother to comply or your other companions. They were the only females who did not, and you respected them in the end. If Pitta does not comply, will you make her your companion too?) Tonie asked.

(Not a bad idea but I don't think your mother will hear of it. I have eighteen companions as it is) he thought.

(She can be your nineteenth father if you approach her the proper way, according to Urb rules and regulations in partnership) she thought, edging.

(You are thinking about eight long rotations before we consummate. I don't have that long) he thought, suddenly sad.

She completely understood her father was near death. He had been keeping it hidden for some time and she didn't want to reveal his secret to her mother, yet.

THE MAN WHO DIDN'T WANT TO GO TO EARTH

(She will find out in due time. Let me tell your mother) he thought.

She only nodded, blanked the screen, and leaned into her black chair and blinked bitter tears. She sat in semi-darkness as view screens moved in and out of sequence, producing information she could use later.

One large Amada Ship suddenly was on top of Faro's ships. It was huge, colored silver and green with brown patches for effect, they began connecting tubes to the smaller ship.

This startled Faro and Tepa who had no time to react since their ship was blind with externals disconnected.

(Your plan of cutting out father failed us, again) Tepa thought.

(*Our plan*) Faro fumed as the trustee sentry stood in green and silver, tall, and ominous with black eyes that clicked.

(You are hereby removed to a prison facility after your talk with Great Can. Do you hereby agree to these terms, or will I be forced to make you comply?) The trustee asked.

They both complied and positioned their hands to be secured behind their backs and a mental contraption on their heads to block thoughts.

The trustee turned to Commander4 and nodded.

(You are in charge) the trustee thought and they vanished in suctioned tubes that merged their bodies into the Amada ship.

Commander4 stared from one sentry to the next, not sure what to do, until another tube connected and Commander1 suctioned into the area.

"I am in charge of this fleet since our leaders are incapacitated according to Article 19," a high-pitched voice came from Commander1. "We will commence to move forward to a rendezvous until further instructions are given. Are there any questions?"

(What happened to your old voice box?) Commander4 asked.

"It was changed," Commander1 replied with a light voice that made eyebrows rise.

Great Can sat in a large chamber of turned stone steps and long tables to support view screens. He sat in green and black robes and his large head supported a black cap that curved to almost cover his thick eyebrows.

Ten other major members of the chamber sat in various spots and stared at the great leader and covered their thoughts so as not to disturb his meditation. Tonna, Shuri, Juni and Nodal were among them.

When the three figures walked in, he knew who they were before he looked up. His white eyes glared as his anger raged against his sons.

Both sons stood with heads bowed, defeated as the trustee robot stood back as Great Can walked in a circle.

(What do you both have to express to me how you failed? Who wants to go first?) Great Can asked.

Tepa remained immobile with his head down and did not flinch, but Faro made a

THE MAN WHO DIDN'T WANT TO GO TO EARTH

movement and struggled with his binds so that the trustee grabbed his arm.

(No, no) Great Can thought (Release their binds. They wouldn't dare try to flee, right?)

The trustee moved his right arm, and the bonds were released together. Faro rubbed his wrists and shifted his head back and forth, but Tepa remained motionless, defeated.

(Faro, since you are the feisty one, tell me what went wrong) Can sat in his chair, but his patience was limited, and Faro knew it.

(This whole obsession for this Pitta lady is what caused this debacle, not us) Faro pointed in the air (Who cares about one lady? We were sent to find the betrayers and Pitta became the point of origin)

Great Can only nodded his head, then turned to Tepa (You agree with his assessment, Tepa?)

Tepa raised his watery eyes and nodded in agreement (But I think it's more than that. It's deeper than Pitta. It's your obsession with everything you cannot have)

(Oh, now I am incompetent. Is that what you are feeling about me?) he stood and growled (I have been in government for over two-hundred long cycles, we have prospered under my tutelage; with the help of betrayer Lin, the great distributor, our lives have increased. I want a little fun and you want to downplay all that I did?)

(Only when it comes to *her*) Tepa thought.

With glaring eyes Can moved close to his son, almost nose to nose (She is way outside your league, son. I can understand your overprotection

THE MAN WHO DIDN'T WANT TO GO TO EARTH

of her, but she is to be broken and used, if not she will gain a position in your life where you have no power)

(Like mother and your other companions?) Faro fumed.

The ten Elders mumbled low and leaned in closer to get a better secretive thought across to their connector. Can was not used to this fury from his sons and was unbalanced and slow in reacting. He felt chagrined as he glanced at the Elders.

(I have companions who do not bow to my will. It's a test of strength. If they win over me, I can release them or they can stay, so it is not about obsession as you think, but a testing of wills) he thought.

When Great Can sat he appeared exhausted.

(You will both have a long time to think about the error of your ways and insubordination. I give a sentence of ten long turns) he waved his arm, and the trustee ushered them from the room.

THE MAN WHO DIDN'T WANT TO GO TO EARTH

21

Faro and Tepa's fleet became one as they moved to Urb at slow speed. When Tonie's green and yellow ship intercepted them, her image was broadcast to all the ships.

(I am now in charge of the entire fleet, per orders from Great Can. Follow me to this point so we can act on a plan to subdue and capture the betrayers) she typed in a location.

"They are not to be killed?" Commander1 asked.

(Captured, not killed) she reiterated (What happened to your voice box? Is it damaged, oh, I see my brother Tepa made some changes. You sound...*different*)

Commander1 tilted his head, confused by her words.

(I will initiate your voice box into our system of thought so you can communicate regularly) she thought.

Within moments his thoughts became a part of the system, but they appeared too high, and a few faces squinted in discomfort, while others smiled at the humor of it.

(That's just as bad as the low grumble) she thought.

I could not sleep and stayed awake as the sun's rays slipped beyond the hills of Jan. I felt we would be all captured, I would be killed, Pitta would be enslaved, and our children placed in a type of foster care or adoption service.

When I felt a hand on my shoulder I almost jumped from my robes, but it was only Pitta.

THE MAN WHO DIDN'T WANT TO GO TO EARTH

(You are really trying to cause both my hearts to stop beating) I thought (Young ones down?)

She only nodded, but I could see the concern on her face and felt angst.

(They found us) I thought.

(I am not sure) she thought.

When she moved me aside and began staring at the screen her mind moved images in and out of focus.

(You are fast at this) I thought.

(Only when I am not tired) she admitted (See, this screen is where a fleet of ships congregated. This is their present position. I believe Tonie is moving to this point at slow speed, which will put her here by daylight)

(I must have missed a chapter somewhere. What happened to the brothers Faro and Tepa?) I asked, when an image showed them in handcuffs (That would explain that)

(They both received ten long turns) she thought.

This took me for a shock, and I stood in silent thought for some time.

(This Tonie, she thinks differently than her brothers. She is subtle) I thought (Her position is outside the planet's rotation at various hidden spots. If we run to another planet, we won't make it due to the quick power of the Authoritarian Ships)

(Even at quick speed) she thought.

I sighed and looked down and thought long and hard, then looked up, defeated. She shook her head negatively.

(No, no) she disagreed.

THE MAN WHO DIDN'T WANT TO GO TO EARTH

(It's the only way. We high tail it to Earth. We need to get through the wormhole without cracks in the central hull or we will come apart at the seams. It's the only way)

She hugged me suddenly and we kissed deeply. I touched her face with both hands. I could feel her doubt about the situation but needed to encourage her as well as myself.

(We will make it) I thought.

Shi was surprised to find so many Authoritarian Ships in hidden spots, that they moved in a gaseous cloud and hoped they were not seen.

(What is with all the ships?) Shi asked.

(Authoritarians are not allowed on Jan due to the unfortunate deaths due to an error in their matrix only on Jan's system. They are banned until it is fixed.

(They are waiting for someone, probably the same people we want to kill) Tor admitted.

(I only want to kill *him*. I have no interest in the others) she admitted.

He stared at her and thought of her words.

(This is the time when you must conclude what is important to you. Revenge or reconciliation?) Tor thought.

She glared at him with steel white eyes.

(What are you communicating?) she asked, irritated.

(We can wait out things, until there is a shootout, possibly be captured, or die; *revenge*, or we can find a quiet place to lay low until things improve. We can abide our time until it is ripe to strike; *reconciliation*) he thought.

She was not agreeable to these words.

(If we travel to Urb and use their high mountains as cover the Authoritarians will not think we are below their noses) Tor presented.

He could tell she was not agreeable with his words, but she grumbled and turned the ship around and floated from hidden spot to hidden spot to the high mountains in Urb.

(We can charge in with guns blasting now, or we can wait for a medium turn) Char pointed out as he flipped a thick round object in his hand.

Char had positioned the ship further back from the wormhole as Authoritarian Ships moved nearby, until a massive Amada ship approached at medium speed.

(Now we are in a bad spot) Char thought.

(Oh no) Ilic thought as he leaned on a chair's backing (Do we have enough firepower to take it out?)

Har moved forward and touched the panel. His face tightened and his eyes glared.

(We have a 446c, the best in cannon and laser fire, able to hold up to twenty individuals fully staffed. We can hold our own, but I am not sure about fighting an Amada ship) Char thought as he peered at the screen and noticed a leak and tried to fix it from his point.

(We have one of the strongest and fastest ships in the galaxy, built for war, but we are no match for an Amada ship, plus extra ships on the side. We will have to play this fast and hard) Har thought.

(We have a leak in the coolant tank. One of our cannons is trashed) Char admitted, frustrated.

THE MAN WHO DIDN'T WANT TO GO TO EARTH

(We can repair it then take the run. We are still going in. No more delays) Har thought.

(I may need help with the tank in case I have to replace it) Char thought as his chair shifted to an open door.

(Take him) Har motioned to Ilic (Make him useful)

Char slid under an extended panel and began to adjust power with his fingers.

(I don't have the strength to do it mentally) he admitted.

(Neither do I) Ilic admitted.

(I will need that refurbished tank, like I thought, this one is shot) Char thought.

Ilic slid him the small tank and took the almost burnt one.

(This one is cooked) Ilic thought as he stared at the burnt holes in its side.

Char went into a quiet mode as Ilic stood and walked in a circle to take in ships that floated in and out of constellations.

(You believe Har will give you up?) Char asked suddenly.

Ilic stopped and turned to Char, but only nodded to agree.

(He has a barter code. If he betrays in a bartering game, he is finished as a barter and trader) Char locked the tank to its hold (You are safe *if* you have the cargo. The moment the cargo is sold on Earth, and it will be sold, because it is none like it in the constellations, you become anathema)

(That's not promising) Ilic thought in angst.

THE MAN WHO DIDN'T WANT TO GO TO EARTH

Char locked panels together, stood and began to synchronize the tank internally.

(It buys you sometime) Char admitted.

22

Geta burned with the passion of revenge and if he could not achieve that he could go for retribution, but when his wife Ceca appeared on the view screen, he was not ready for stories of forgiveness and he disconnected her line.

He knew he would pay for that action sometime in the future with her words of anger and betrayal, but he didn't care. He wanted his pound of flesh and more from Ilic.

(They are out here somewhere) Geta thought as his nervous long fingers intertwined.

(We will have to return for repairs. Our energies are unstable, and we are low on power) Sentry18 admitted.

(Damn) Geta grumbled (Turn her around for repairs and make it fast)

(Too good to be true) Pitta thought to me as I hovered behind her (There has been a stop effect against the Authoritarians on Jan since two long turns ago. I totally forget about that)

I thought as I sat next to her (That's why they didn't come on the planet, they would have been fired upon)

(Some robots went haywire. Janeites don't trust them anymore) she thought.

(How can we use that to our advantage?) I asked.

(It's been already used. If it wasn't for the stop effect, we would be imprisoned or dead) she thought.

(So, if we leave the planet we are done. If we stay, we remain trapped) I rubbed my face with

THE MAN WHO DIDN'T WANT TO GO TO EARTH

both hands (I need a break and shower or I will be done)
    I climbed in the shower and began to enjoy the hot water on my tired body. When I opened my eyes, I was startled, because she stood before me, silent. She smiled under the water, and I reciprocated. We stood this way for a long time as the hot water poured on our naked bodies.

(We don't know how long they will hide in Jan; we may need to motivate them to leave. You cannot go there) she turned to the sentries (but I can, but I will need a proper ship that is not Authoritarian)
    She stared from screen to screen (Maybe I can commandeer the one that appears hiding. Stun their circuits) she thought.

    Shi felt a triumph in almost making it near Urb to settle down and lie low, but Tor reminded her to brace for a stun ray!
    (What?) she asked.
    Sudden explosions erupted her thinking as she fell to the floor, dazed.
    Circuits exploded and smoke simmered in certain spots. Tor was dazed and leaned back in his chair as a hose was suctioned to the ship and Tonie appeared carrying a laser weapon with three sentries.
    (Look what we have here, jackpot) Tonie thought.
    (I thought the brothers would catch us) Shi thought (Not the likes of you)

THE MAN WHO DIDN'T WANT TO GO TO EARTH

When Shi rose to rush her, Tonie stepped to the side and Shi stumbled into a bulkhead and slid down, unconscious.

(Unlike my brothers I hate violence, most of the time) Tonie smiled (Secure them in a back room while we repair the ship for a rendezvous on Jan)

We awakened the young ones before the sun rose to make a break to Earth. They were excited and afraid at the same time. I wrapped them in a material to protect them against debris or other foreign objects.

(You need one too, father) Hut thought.
(And you, mother) Nesh pointed out.
(There are only two of them and two of you) Pitta replied (We will be all right)

We all hurried to a nearby elevator that took us below at moderate speed. As the lift lowered, we could see across from us another elevator rose, and our hearts froze.

It was Tonie and three sentries!

Tonie tried to stop the elevated platform, but it was forced to go to the floor they pushed, before it lowered too slowly. She cursed and fumed as Lin's ship rose quickly and vanished into the sky.

(Follow them) she roared like an animal as her thoughts almost came in jumbles.

Shi began to slowly recover in a back room, strapped in beige secures. When she looked over, she saw Tor, awakened, almost struggling.

(Save your strength. They are almost impregnable. I know because I helped design

THE MAN WHO DIDN'T WANT TO GO TO EARTH

them. We used them on Urb to transfer undesirables to their hearings with the judge) she admitted.

He cursed silently and looked around for anything to free them, anything...

(Extreme temperature changes can give us a chance. I am assuming I still have some control of the ship. Ship, through focused response to me, only, do I have Environment Control?) she asked.

(Yes) the ship responded.

Shi closed her eyes and calmly demanded that controls be increased to maximum.

(This will be detrimental to the flesh) the ship thought.

(Do it) Shi commanded (Then decrease Environment Controls quite the opposite)

(Damn, it is hot in here) Tonie thought as she mentally moved controls around (Environment is off-line, what?)

When the Environment Control shifted to midway the temperature became tolerable but then it became extremely cold, so cold she could see her breath.

(What the hell?) she asked, confused.

(Environment Control is offline, *again*) sentry14 admitted.

In a far back-room Shi and Tor struggled with their secures until they began to break and snap as if brittle. Tor was exhilarated and surprised at the same time.

(I didn't think it would work. It was theoretical) Shi thought.

(Now it's fact) Tor looked around for weapons (We have no weapons to confront them)

THE MAN WHO DIDN'T WANT TO GO TO EARTH

(We make do with what we have) Shi thought.

Tor looked around and saw metal, disconnected pipes in the corner. Usually, they were used to repair conduits, but he took a few in his hand and tossed a few to her.

(We make do) Tor thought.

23

I was concerned they would catch us in the 229t ship style, which was an average travel and family flyer able to hold up to ten individuals.

When I took off, I looked back to notice they had a 446b, a medium class ship with laser guns able to hold up to 20 individuals and built for fast travel and air battles.

(Matter of fact I think that was Shi's ship) I looked back at Pitta who sat forward (What would Tonie be doing with Shi's ship?)

Pitta looked confused as Hut sat tensely at my side. Nesh sat to the far left, strapped in the chair in case of turbulence or air battles.

(We are breaking through the atmosphere. I don't know what we are about to see. Visuals and audio are scrambled. The moment we are clear we are running) I admitted as my two hearts increased in rhythm.

(To Earth) Hut clarified.

(What the hell is going on with the Environment Controls?) Tonie asked, exasperated (I have no time for this shit)

Then, Great Can's face appeared above her. She was startled and cursed through pursed lips.

(Father, you need to give me a warning before you do that) she thought.

(I see you have not caught her, *yet*) he thought.

(We are in pursuit. I just need a little time) she thought, aggravated by his intrusion.

THE MAN WHO DIDN'T WANT TO GO TO EARTH

(Do I have to do everything myself?) he asked (On Urb Cis had denied me with help from the rough man; now my own family is denying Pitta what I could have achieved through Cis) he thought.

(Who is *Cis* and this rough man denial? I don't know what you are talking about, father) she admitted.

(It's a long story so I will not elaborate. I have already commissioned one Amada and will be there shortly for my prize) he thought.

(What?) she shifted screen images around (I already have an Amada ship covering the wormhole to Earth)

(That's the one I commissioned. It was doing nothing, so I gave it something to do. That's what leaders do. They commission things)

She bowed her head in frustration and sighed (I needed that ship to stop any run on the wormhole)

(I don't care about the wormhole or Earth. I care about Pitta, the rough man girl. Be there shortly, daughter) he thought.

(This is highly irregular, father. You cannot abandon the chair in case of a coup. Urb Law is whoever sits in the chair stays for ten long rotations) she thought in angst.

(My ambitious sons are locked away. Who will want this chair, but them?) he only smiled mischievously.

She waited until his image faded away like smoke so that he would not see inside of her mind or heart.

THE MAN WHO DIDN'T WANT TO GO TO EARTH

Great Can took a small ship to a large Amada ship, piloted by the trustee who appeared to smile, but its lips usually remained straight, as the great leader stood next to him.

(Take her ahead at quick speed) Can ordered as he sat in a long, silver-backed chair.

(Quick speed) the trustee agreed and complied.

(The Environment Controls are returning to their normal perimeters) Sentry19 thought.

(Wonder what that was about?) Tonie asked, bemused, until she turned and saw Shi and Tor with pipes in their hands for battle.

(I have no time for this shit) Tonie thought.

(Intruders) Sentry17 thought, but it barely came out as a thought when Tor struck him in the head with many blows.

Tonie hurried into the next room and began to try and secure the ship and contact Urb at the same time.

In the next room Shi ran a pipe through the Sentry19 and turned it so that his laser weapon simmered and fell into misuse. When she finished it off with two kicks to the neck it fell backward, broken and simmering.

Tor battled with Sentry16 and when it crashed face down and did not move Tor and Shi knew the ship was secured, except for one individual in a sealed room.

They walked to the door and peered in and were surprised when the door unsealed. Tor went first, carefully, he aimed the pipe as Shi followed with her pipe raised.

THE MAN WHO DIDN'T WANT TO GO TO EARTH

(I'm not armed) Tonie admitted as she sat in a long brown chair with raised arms (I did what I really wanted to do, so I don't care anymore)

Shi stared at various screens trying to figure what did she do?

(I started a process that will free everyone from the claws of my father) she faintly smiled (You want your freedom, right? My father has left his chair leaderless. We have a law that says whoever takes the chair takes it for ten long rotations. You are free. I don't care about the betrayer rebellion)

(You cannot take the chair from here) Tor thought.

(It's not me who is taking the chair this instant) she thought.

Tepa on Urb was instantly released from his bonds. He saw the overhead thought blocker as it shifted forward, and lost power and his shackles collapsed like butter.

He stood, startled for some time, before he realized he was free as a nearby door shifted over and his brother Faro walked in.

(Sister has freed us. Robots are on our side. Let's get what's coming to us) Faro thought.

Slowly, Tepa, down and defeated, saw hope in a hopeless situation and smiled broadly.

We broke through the atmosphere and hidden ships advanced with laser fire. I barely dodged them and quick-speeded to the wormhole.

(I don't know if we are going to make it) I thought as I maneuvered the ship (Ship protect the inner-most core)

THE MAN WHO DIDN'T WANT TO GO TO EARTH

(This will leave the other parts of the ship vulnerable, father) Hut thought, frightened.

(If we don't protect the inner core, we won't make it through the wormhole) I thought.

I could visualize the ship with tiny hands that tightened around the main core as we moved at quick speed with many ships in pursuit.

(The Amada is gone) Ilic thought.

(That's to our advantage) Char thought as he moved his hand around to balance the ship.

(It's now or never) Har thought as he prepared the 446c which was fitted with lasers and cannons and could hold up to twenty individuals (Ready cannons and lasers)

(Laser and cannons ready) Char thought.

They were suddenly struck from behind with laser fire. Sparks and smoke billowed about the ship as Har growled and peered into the rear view.

(Your friend is back) Har thought as Char turned the ship about.

(My friend?) Ilic asked, then he sighed and dropped his head in frustration.

Geta growled as he received fire and laser cannon from the much larger ship. He banged his dark hand on the panel and returned fire, but the robot sentries, worried, reminded him they were outgunned.

(We cannot take much more) Sentry18 admitted.

(Back off) Geta commanded.

(They are backing off) Char admitted.

THE MAN WHO DIDN'T WANT TO GO TO EARTH

(Let's get to that wormhole before more problems abound) Har thought.
(The Amada is back) Ilic thought in angst.
Har growled like an animal with fists balled.
(Take it to them) Har commanded (I aim the cannons Char, you the aim the lasers, fire)

The trustee held on the silver panel as it shifted back and forth from explosions. Sentries looked from panel to panel and tried to balance the ship as Great Can held onto his chair.
(Return fire) Great Can commanded.
Laser and cannon fire erupted through space with such yield miniature explosions came from debris as Char tried to maneuver, but damaged cracks began to form.
(Protect the core and maneuver with the least eruptions and return fire) Har commanded.

Geta moved his ship further back just when Ceca, his partner's face appeared on the view screen. She looked most displeased.
They had been married for over eighty long rotations, but this was one time he really did not have time...
(Not now Ceca) he thought (I just need to regroup. I am so close)
(Is it worth it? You have five sons and two daughters. What is this cargo worth if you are dead?) she asked.
Her words jolted him, and he lost focus and did not see debris from the battle ahead. The sentries tried to maneuver around the flaming metal, but it was too late.

The flaming debris acted as a sheath and had cut through their ship like butter. The remainder of the ship exploded and took out a nearby Authoritarian ship. These eruptions caused a bright light that cascaded through the darkness.

Har noticed this interchange and backed off from the fight to regroup.
(Your friend is no more) Har thought (Now the Amada and its ships)
Ilic bowed his head as he collapsed in a chair and tears flowed for his friend.
(Our power is almost gone. We may have to regroup to recharge) Char warned.
(In, in) Har balled his fists to punch the thought.
Two authoritarian ships erupted so that debris crashed into the Amada. This caused nominal damage as the trustee turned to Great Can.
(We are not trashed. We have sufficient energy to finish the fight) the trustee bragged.
(Finish them) Great Can commanded.

24

(Engines are taxed, minimal damage, the core is strong, balanced) Pitta thought.

(Wormhole ahead, count down entered) Hut thought.

(Going in) I thought.

(There is a major battle ahead, the Amada and some other ships) Hut thought.

(Won't stop in time) I thought.

Nesh screamed as we all yelled in unison as the wormhole opened...

(Damn) Char thought (I can't pull back in time)

(Go through them) Har growled.

(We are all dead) Ilic gripped the chair as his pink knuckles turned white with pressure.

The trustee's eyes widened, and his eyebrows rose on seeing the incoming ships, it turned to Great Can, concerned about their survival. Great Can stood and wobbled to a nearby panel.

(Oh no) was his last thought.

The Amada was cut in half as two ships entered the wormhole, pulled by immense light and energy. The other ships erupted in flames as they tried to pull back and their engines collapsed. Fire engulfed the wormhole and cascaded out.

Great Can opened his mouth as fire engulfed the ship and burned through much of the hull. His body disintegrated with a painful scream as the trustee stared, blank-faced and began to melt from the intense heat.

I wasn't sure if we were going to make it to the other side, but when we emerged from light and energy, we all yelled in unison as we saw the Earth in its beauty with land masses and water.

Various satellites could be seen, also a variety of ships hovered, their inhabitants probably watching our quick descent above Earth's atmosphere.

Pitta stared at her daughter and nodded to reassure her that all was going to be all right. Nesh stared, frightened with a face filled with tears and rose to remove the straps that protected her.

(Repairs) I sat in a moving chair that turned and began to look for damage.

(Multiple ruptures and cracks in the frame) Hut typed in information (We won't be going anywhere for some time)

(Let's start on those repairs) I demanded (So we won't burn up in Earth's entry)

(That's what the pods are for) Pitta admitted.

Able to take up to five-thousand degrees the pods were only used for emergencies of extreme heat or cold.

(You don't want to use the pods if you don't need to) I thought.

When immense light and energy moved from the wormhole it almost blinded us temporarily. I blinked almost in slow motion as a hidden ship approached.

(Father, we have a problem) Hut thought, alarmed (It's another ship and it's not stopping)

(What?) I asked, confused.

(Stop the ship) Har thought in angst.

THE MAN WHO DIDN'T WANT TO GO TO EARTH

(Controls are compromised) Char shifted his long fingers about (We are trashed)

Ilic stared at the view screen with wild white eyes as they crashed into the smaller ship and minor explosions came from each structure.

(Get as close to the Earth as possible or our pods will float in space, and we will be lost) Har demanded.

(I cannot disconnect from the other ship. We are going in hot) Char thought.

(We will lose the cargo) Ilic screamed in frustration.

(Who cares about the cargo? Can't use the cargo if we are dead) Char rose and walked to a pod, slid in and closed the clear container so that it became opaque.

Ilic hurried to a pod as Har stood next to one and hesitated to climb in. Ilic gestured for him to climb in.

(We will make it) Ilic encouraged.

(That is the most positive thing you thought about this entire trip) Har thought.

Ilic smiled, touched a button and the container closed and became opaque. Har cursed, climbed in and looked around before making it opaque.

(She was such a fine ship) Har thought.

(Now we must use the pods) I thought, reluctantly to Pitta.

Nesh was released from her straps as Pitta guided her to a silver container as Hut argued to stay and navigate the ship.

(The ship is gone) I thought (We can use the pods to get to Earth. There are homing beacons to

THE MAN WHO DIDN'T WANT TO GO TO EARTH

take us to the nearest alien colony, away from most Humans. We will go from there)

(I'm sorry, father) Hut's white eyes teared up and he hugged me.

(You did nothing wrong) I told him.

Hut slid into the pod, and it became opaque as I turned to Nesh, and her pod became dark. I looked at Pitta.

(Your turn) I thought.

(See you on the other side) Pitta smiled and slid into her pod and it became dark.

I was suddenly filled with terror. As the connected ships burned and entered Earth's atmosphere, I saw what Nesh and Pitta saw, a ship that crashed into another ship.

If what they saw was true, then there was a high probability that what my son and I saw could be true. The monster with two heads stomped around to devour…

THE MAN WHO DIDN'T WANT TO GO TO EARTH

<u>EXPECTATIONS OF BEING ON A NEW WORLD</u>

THE MAN WHO DIDN'T WANT TO GO TO EARTH

CHUCK PALAHNIUK QUOTE
"What makes Earth feel like hell is our expectation that it should feel like heaven."
DAMNED

THE MAN WHO DIDN'T WANT TO GO TO EARTH

25

Mars was not sure what happened. He slowly emerged from the tubing after 22 minutes of inactivity. He knew the system was designed to check for environmental pressures, fires, rain, and could assess when the best time was to emerge.

Mars vs Mars

    I was totally confused as I laid in the tube for some time as its door suctioned back. I knew the monster with two heads would devour me and my family...speaking of family. I forced my body up to search for Hut, Nesh and Pitta; but a kind hand pushed me back.

    I knew the tubes were designed to go to the nearest land mass, so I was not surprised to be looking at trees that stood tall. On our planet they were called *Shonna*.

    (Help is arriving. We saw your signal from afar but didn't think you would arrive so quickly) the dark-skinned Fuman thought.

    (You can throw thoughts) I thought, surprised.

    (Are you surprised I can throw thoughts or surprised because we can throw thoughts on Earth?) he asked.

    (On Earth) I thought, then he helped me from the tube.

    (I'm Arn2) he shook my hand (Here are your family and friends, all doing well)

    I could not turn fast enough to hug Hut, Nesh and Pitta. Nesh suddenly became sick and vomited near a tree or a Shonna, while Hut rubbed her back and tried to comfort her.

THE MAN WHO DIDN'T WANT TO GO TO EARTH

(The process of the cocktail and your violent entry) Arn2 thought.

Then I saw three more individuals I did not recognize who emerged from the tubes, but Pitta's body language said she knew the individuals.

(Ilic, again) she growled (Master Har, my emotional/thought blocking teacher and his friend Char. I believe they are the reason this all happened)

(We have an air vehicle waiting to take you to base and give you a full medical examination, then we can go from there) Arn2 pointed to a gray and yellow vehicle that waited with engines humming.

(Which country are we in?) Hut asked, excitedly.

(Guatemala) Arn2 admitted.

Hut looked confused and thought of the history and people of Guatemala. I was pleased we had all survived as we climbed into the vehicle and was strapped in, but Pitta was on edge the whole flight as she fumed about *Ilic*.

I really could not figure what hold he had on her; but it was not my concern. I was grateful we had all survived despite some nausea and dizziness.

We were all unbalanced emotionally about the traumatic entry, but Arn2 was a great host and placed us in conjoining rooms so that we had connections with Hut and Nesh; but still retained some privacy.

(I noticed he placed us together. You don't mind?) I asked, unsure.

THE MAN WHO DIDN'T WANT TO GO TO EARTH

(We crashed your party. I am pleased he saw that we were a couple. We are a couple, eh?) she smiled slyly at me, but motioned with her hand (You don't have to answer that)

(I'm not obligated?) I asked.

She smiled and bowed her head.

Har and Ilic were the most anxious when they could not see the cargo from their point. Char vomited near a large rock and Arn2 gave him a sweet drink that settled his stomach immediately.

(We could sell this on my planet and gain a fortune) Char thought as he stared at the cup and was pleased as his insides settled, but squinted when his hand caused pain in movement (What is it?)

(Clear soda mixed with stomach settlers) Arn2 thought with a smile.

(Are you the rough man's son?) Har asked (You are Arn) Har drank back the soda mixture (I thought you had died in a gunfight)

(I did. I am his clone) Arn2 thought in a matter-of-fact thought (I am technically I am called Arn2 to distinguish from the first Arn)

Har, Char and Ilic stared, in awe, but Arn2 took it all in stride.

(Your vehicle awaits. You will be taken to the base and given a medical examination and released to rest. In the morning you will have a meeting with Lady Asia about your next step) Arn2 thought.

(Do you know what happened to our cargo?) Ilic asked as he hovered under the tall Fuman (I am sure it survived. We placed it in an impregnable container...) Ilic was moved to the side by Har.

THE MAN WHO DIDN'T WANT TO GO TO EARTH

(Pay him no mind. He is delirious. Who cares about cargo in a mad crash across the world? We will take the air vehicle, rest and meet this Asia, person) Har thought.

(We barely survived ourselves who cares about some cargo?) Char asked and led Ilic to the air vehicle with such force he almost fell face forward.

(Watch it) Ilic thought, aggravated.

(*You* watch it) Char thought.

26

Aisha had a healthy girl named Aila and still contended with matters Other Worldly Alien. <u>Mars vs Mars</u>

Despite some scratches Ilic was okay, but Char had a fractured wrist, possibly from the landing and he was quickly healed by technology that hummed with light and frequency. Har stared, not surprised.

(Compliments of the blues) Har thought.

(Better known as the Harmonic Aliens on our planet) Ilic thought.

When they were placed in adjoining rooms they decided to meet on an extended balcony. Har was not sure if microphones were active.

(We must be extra careful of our intentions. We don't know if the cargo was destroyed, or if it survived. I know Asia from my last Earth excursion. I can contact her and get a feel if they found it or not) Har thought.

(Do you trust this Asia lady?) Char asked as he nervously flipped a thick coin with various colors that reflected off overhead lights.

(How did you know she was addressed as Lady Asia on Earth?) Har asked, curious.

(I didn't. It was a lucky guess) Char thought with a smile.

(She is like an ambassador between Earthlings and aliens. She is also the lady friend of rough man Mars.' She had a daughter through him) Har thought with a smile (She is trustworthy)

(This Mars guy gets around) Ilic thought with a smile as he thought about the many female

THE MAN WHO DIDN'T WANT TO GO TO EARTH

companions, he could achieve. Har and Char smiled at Ilic's thoughts that came freely.

(You will never be like him, don't even think about it) Char thought and patted his arm roughly (I owe you an apology. You were exposing the cargo)

(I will be extra careful next time) Ilic thought.

(Let's get some rest and have our meet with Asia in the morning) Har thought, but he shielded his thoughts and emotions so well they did not know he had no intentions of sleeping, yet.

He wanted to use his private time to search for the cargo and take it all for himself.

I slept until the sun rose and that was not by much. I still felt groggy as I laid next to Pitta who looked vulnerable with eyes closed and mouth pressed. I knew she was sharp as nails and could wake up in seconds and not be groggy, me on the other hand...

I staggered to a nearby yellow bathroom (on Urb they are called *wash areas)* and proceeded to relieve myself in a toilet. On Urb it's called *flush away* and washed my face with hand rags and dried them with towels of blue and green.

When I emerged, Pitta wobbled past me and hurried into the bathroom to vomit. I smiled.

(Weakling) I thought.

(I read that) she thought.

I only snickered to keep the humor going.

(Today we meet Lady Aisha) I thought.

(She wants to examine our intentions) she thought, and walked from the bathroom to adjust into clean clothes of gold and yellow (If we are considered dangerous, we will be stored

THE MAN WHO DIDN'T WANT TO GO TO EARTH

somewhere for a long time, the children will go into foster care for other worldly aliens)

She slid an image toward me of all the information she collected about Lady Aisha.

(Also, she is no lady, but a Phasee from the first Phasees, but the word lady is used for respect and to lessen fear) she thought.

(Why should they fear her?) I asked, confused.

(She is not Human) Pitta thought.

I stared, worried this could turn upside down for us quickly.

I stood in an open area of bodies that moved from point to point in various-colored robes, as Hut and Nesh smiled from all the activity. It resembled a food court with small tables, chairs and well lit.

Bolaris, Fumans, Phasees, and Humans moved about and acknowledged each other's presence without conflict. Hut and Nesh marveled at the combination of races and how they worked in unison.

(I want to try Chinese food, first) Hut thought as he pointed to a vendor with a line of interested bodies.

(Never heard of it) I thought.

(That's because you didn't study Earth culture like Nesh and I did) Hut admitted.

Nesh smiled with a nod of her head.

(You must be careful of certain combinations of foods here. They might not appeal to our palate) Pitta warned.

(Stick to the vegan, organic side you should be all right) I thought.

THE MAN WHO DIDN'T WANT TO GO TO EARTH

When I noticed Lady Aisha, it was almost immediate. She stood tall, confident of her abilities to keep the races in harmony, and not looking like she was nearly 300 years-of-age.

Aila, who was near 9 years young, had tanned, brown skin, blonde hair, gray eyes and a nice smile. When she extended her hand, we were all pleased by her politeness.

(I am Aila) she thought.

I shook her hand and Hut and Nesh shook her hand as well. Pitta was put off by all the smiles and she appeared aloof and peered left and right as if she expected another attack as what happened on past planets.

(This place is well fortified) Aisha thought as she picked up Pitta's nervous energy (Shall we sit and talk?)

Lady Aisha felt to leave her daughter in a well-protected apartment while she interviewed Har and his constituents. She was not sure of their intentions and took two tall Phasees garbed in blue, white and gold with electrified spears.

(No need for security) Har hugged her warmly (Have not seen you in near one-hundred long turns)

(Near ninety years here) she smiled (You can never tell with foreigners from different worlds, you know the drill, Har, just being careful. I still cannot read you well, master at hiding your true emotions; but these two fellas I can read like a book)

Ilic and Char stood nervous in black and yellow robes. Aisha walked closer, then turned to Har.

THE MAN WHO DIDN'T WANT TO GO TO EARTH

(Where's the cargo?) she asked.

Har looked skyward, frustrated, exposed, while Ilic shook his head side to side and Char stared to the side, afraid to look forward into her perceptive white eyes.

(You don't know where it is at) she admitted (How interesting. Were you going to place it through customs or find a nefarious way around it, I cannot tell. The ship mishap almost destroyed your plan of making a bunch of money)

(Of course, we were going to go through customs. It would have been a legitimate business transaction, if it survived) Har argued.

(It survived) she thought.

Har was surprised she could hide that fact from him. He knew she was as agile at hiding emotions and thoughts than he could ever be. He tried to contain his excitement at knowing the cargo survived.

(When can we see it?) Ilic asked.

(Now) she admitted.

Har stood with Char and Ilic with eyes that gleamed with excitement as Aisha stared in horror and the two tall Phasees behind stared with great concern.

Below them were two large containers, scratched, scuffed, and burned on the outside, but undamaged on the inside.

Inside were creatures, unmoving with eyes closed, with two heads opposite each other, long arms, long legs. They appeared to be eight feet tall with various rows of teeth near the head. Their skin was a thick fabric with mini scales and almost a bluish green.

THE MAN WHO DIDN'T WANT TO GO TO EARTH

(What the hell is it?) she asked, alarmed.

THE MAN WHO DIDN'T WANT TO GO TO EARTH

27

(It is a Security Sentry4681 better known as a SS4681, developed by my company and a friend who is now dead...) thought Ilic, sadly.

(What does it do, scare you to death?) Aisha asked as she felt a chill up her spine.

(Close) Ilic stepped forward, excited to explain his idea (It is designed to chase down burglars and place them in handcuffs until the proper authorities arrive)

She was totally shocked for a moment and turned to the lifeless monsters, then back to Ilic. Ilic raised his hands to stop her confused thoughts.

(It looks dangerous, but it's not able to cause violence. That's what makes it so original. Robbers and the like do not need to know it's not designed to cause violence, by the time the truth is out there I will pull back the sentries) Ilic thought.

(We will have made a ton of money by then) Char thought.

(Foolproof) Har thought with a sly smile.

Aisha looked from face to face and did not depict any deception even with Har's blocking techniques. She felt he was sincere at this point and nodded to reassure them.

(I will take this matter up with Earth's Barter and Trade Council in the morning. They will want a demonstration, so prepare yourselves) she thought.

Ilic and Char smiled as Har nodded and hugged her. Soon she was gone, and they marveled at their possible way out of poverty.

THE MAN WHO DIDN'T WANT TO GO TO EARTH

(Ilic and his friends are only a few doors from us) Pitta thought, worried.

I finally had a chance to sit down and eat Chinese food, but it was only in small doses. I found it to be heavy and greasy, so I stopped, sat back and found a biscuit from a separate bucket called: *chicken*.

(Who cares?) I projected (His world is not our world)

(There you are wrong. Already they changed our lives with this ship crash, which I and Nesh dreamed about, thank you) she admitted.

Nesh helped Hut eat some of his food, so he nudged her, and she smiled and chewed from her own plate.

(Only through chemicals in the system. When the chemicals wear off you see nothing when it comes to the future) I thought.

(Maybe there is some truth to that, but your seeing did not manifest. Where is the monster with two heads?) Pitta asked.

Lady Aisha seemed to appear as if a ghost behind us. I was instantly startled.

(I know where it's at) Lady Aisha replied.

I stopped eating and lost my appetite immediately as Hut and Nesh stared, horrified with the words from Lady Aisha.

We converged in the apartment area for privacy as we sat in terrified silence with our thoughts closed as Aisha explained a new system designed by Ilic and Geta.

(If it works it can revolutionize the security system across the solar system and beyond) Aisha thought.

(Whatever he places his hands on will become a disaster. I know him. He had so many fears and failures he almost caused more disasters when dealing with Mars and the Fumans) Pitta remembered.

(I want to give them a chance. Of course, safety protocols will be placed, just in case) Lady Aisha thought.

(It will not be enough) Pitta stood and left the room, angered.

Lady Aisha only nodded and frowned, but wanted to change the negative to a positive, so gathered her thoughts and smiled broadly.

(I don't know how long you want to stay on Earth, but if you have enough interjections to stay healthy, you are cleared to travel) Lady Aisha thought to raise our spirits.

(We have enough for two medium turns) I interjected.

(That's less than two weeks) Lady Aisha thought (Your abrupt landing fell into the sea and did not kill any individuals, so you are free to do what you want. Try to enjoy yourselves. You deserve it)

(I was concerned about the landing too) I thought (I know the pods are positioned to go to land, but the damaged ship...)

(We have projected signals in place in cases of this type and all destroyed craft are positioned over the sea, unless you crush some boats with people in them, then we can't have that, can we?) she asked.

I silently nodded and tried to contain my worries. We all stared at each other but remained

THE MAN WHO DIDN'T WANT TO GO TO EARTH

silent in our fear of a monster with two heads and able to tear us to shreds.

Pitta sat at a small table and drank from an orange "smoothie," her favorite food on Earth, so far. She was reluctant to try anything else, yet, and wanted to stick to non-processed, organically grown foods.

From her position she could see one-hundred and eighty degrees and saw Aisha as she walked with two security Phasee personnel.

Then, she noticed Har and Char as they walked together. She gripped the chair when she saw Ilic, her anger and fear rose, and she stood. Ilic noticed her, backed up and hurried into a nearby room.

Char and Har looked confused, not sure what was going on. She held back in a crowd of people and they, confused, left Ilic to find food to eat.

She smiled as a plan began to form in her mind. She knew she had to act now, or all would be lost...

28

Ilic was terrified of her. He fell over some objects and barely stood in the dimly lit area. He could sense her nearby, but where? When he tried to contact Char and Har on a small message board he could not find it...

(Looking for this?) it was her thoughts and he looked at her to his right, but it was too late to get away, as she jabbed him in the jaw, he fell like a bag of rocks, unconscious.

(Easy prey) she thought with a sly smile.

(Where in the Urb is this individual at?) Char asked as he eyed his wrist dials.

(Go find out if he wants to talk and eat or wants to do something else) Har demanded, irritated (I am tempted to cast him to the wind, he has been more trouble than he is worth)

(We need his codes to operate the beasts) Char thought.

(I already have the codes) Har thought.

Char sat, amazed and confused at the same time.

(I achieved his codes on the first meeting. Can't tell him that. He must seem useful, until we are well into making money, then he can be disposed of) Har thought.

Char looked, surprised and horrified of killing his friend of ten long turns.

(I don't mean to kill him, you idiot. Remove him from the program so we can gain the spoils) Har motioned him away to find Ilic, impatient by the whole exchange.

THE MAN WHO DIDN'T WANT TO GO TO EARTH

(Okay, you will tell me how to destroy the things) Pitta sat close to his front as he blinked back pain.

(What?) he asked, confused.

(I will throttle you with more fists. Follow my words carefully. How do you destroy *the things*?) she asked, sensing he was holding back vital information.

(I don't have a destruct button; I just turn it off) he thought, hoping that was enough.

(Everything has a weakness, Ilic. How do you kill it?) she asked.

(Just turn things off. They are not organic. They don't breathe and cannot be killed, but there is a shutdown button. They are also self-generating if damaged) he thought.

(Almost invincible, you idiot. Why would you build something that cannot be killed?) she growled.

(Robbers and thieves could use violence against them. I did not want to include violence in their system but made them impregnable so they could catch the robbers and thieves) he surmised.

She held back from throttling him with blows and only shook her head negatively.

(They are not built to cause violence. You have the wrong idea) he thought.

(Take me to them) she thought.

(It's under heavy guard) he thought.

(I don't care) she thought.

When they carefully walked from the room and into various crowds as she held his arm, he felt as if he was walking to his death.

THE MAN WHO DIDN'T WANT TO GO TO EARTH

Char arrived at the room and looked around. He found it odd that things were overturned, and two chairs faced each other, and one had straps for restraints.

He pulled up his view screen and contacted Har immediately.

(We may have a problem) Char thought.

For better security the beasts were kept far from prying eyes in a containment area that was well lit and heavily guarded with tall Phasees in black and green robes, electrified spears and white piercing eyes.

She knew they could scan deeper and faster than most Phasees on Earth; but she had an advantage: *Ilic*.

She knew the record of his former arrival with friends would be noted, so he forced a smile and tried not to appear apprehensive.

As they moved closer to the Phasee guards, she smiled, used her blocking technique so they would not read her thoughts and stunned them with a stun grenade.

As they collapsed to the floor Ilic stared down at them, not sure how to take present events.

Then she pressed her hand against the dialing keys until the door opened. He looked shocked.

(Now you know how I got into your room) she thought as she pushed him in.

(Please, don't do this. I have not prepared the beasts for the technology in this region. They must be vetted) he made a yell from his mouth.

THE MAN WHO DIDN'T WANT TO GO TO EARTH

(Shut the hell up. We are not trying to vet anything we only want to shut them down, permanently) she thought.

Har stood in the room and looked around, confused why someone would kidnap Ilic.
(He's useless) Har thought.
(Not so) Char typed in commands and watched visuals appear of them in two chairs (Watch their lips)
Har stared with pointed eyes.
(She is asking about *the things*?) Har asked.
(She wants to sabotage the beasts. She hates Ilic and wants to destroy him. We must get to her before she destroys our cash hole) Char looked around for a weapon.
(There are no weapons allowed in the area. We will have to tackle her without any extra help) Har thought.
(I don't think we can do it. She whipped the rough man's ass, and he gave her a baby, she whipped him so bad) Char thought.
Har looked at Char, disbelieving it all.
(True story) Char thought.
Har did not want to respond to that silliness and walked hurriedly to the containment area to confront his pupil in training, while Char followed reluctantly with wide eyes filled of terror.

(Where is your mother?) I asked Nesh as I looked from one view screen to another.
(She went for a walk. She does that when she is upset. Helps her clear her head) Nesh thought as she played Earth games called *cards* on screens to match numbers.

THE MAN WHO DIDN'T WANT TO GO TO EARTH

(You should play some games with us, father) Hut thought as he moved cards around mentally.
(No, I want to make sure Pitta is fine before I do anything else) I thought, then I walked into a busy walkway of bodies and moving robots that carried bags.
Then, Hut and Nesh were on each side of me with faint smiles.
(We will go with you to find her) they thought in unison.
I only nodded and smiled at them in approval and began to move about in a minor search that brought anxiety to my heart.

Pitta and Ilic moved about the room as small alarms began to sound. She sealed the room and disabled the cameras with a wave of her hand.
(Same tech as the Harmonic Aliens, easy to disable, not built for security but communication) she thought.
She stood with Ilic and peered around, trying to figure out the major buttons to shoot them into space.
(You want to send them back into space?) he asked, alarmed.
(I don't think they would survive, do you, without the proper tech and charging generators, just need to find) he shoved her and ran so that she was stunned.
(When I catch you, I will kill you) she fumed.
(Have to catch me, then) he thought and hid under various desks and chairs and tried to make himself go silent so she could not find his thoughts and keep her word and kill him.

29

As Nesh, Hut and I walked around the area to search for Pitta, Lady Aisha approached us with deep concern in her eyes.

(We have a serious problem) Lady Aisha thought (Follow me)

Way far in the back of the area where the lighting began to fade, we saw two Phasee guards sprawled on the floor as other guards moved their hands over them so that consciousness was achieved.

(Stay for a moment) one guard projected to this friend.

(This way) Lady Aisha and the rest of us gathered up short steps and ended on a promenade that looked down (She found a way to disable our cameras, but she cannot fade out the windows)

We were fifty feet above the action below as Pitta walked around, trying to find Ilic. Next to her were two long beasts, unmoving in long tubes that appeared damaged from the crash.

(This is not good) I thought as I recognized my dream.

(It's the dream come true) Hut thought, terrified.

(I believe she lost her catch) Lady Aisha thought.

(Mother) Nesh thought, anguished.

(Let me talk her down) I offered.

(You can try but you only have a few moments before I send in the Area Guard. She is without a hostage, and they can take her quicker this way) she thought.

THE MAN WHO DIDN'T WANT TO GO TO EARTH

I turned and saw several soldiers who were waiting with dark masks, laser weapons and dark gray suits. I then knew this could get *bad*.

Lady Aisha presented me with a fitted pad against certain injuries. At first, I refused, but she insisted, and I wrapped it around my torso so that it moved and fitted to my features. I was also given a green helmet.

(Just in case) she thought (You have five minutes)

I patted Hut and Nesh on the head, hugged them and proceeded on the platform, walked into a bubble that lowered me to the floor.

Automatically Pitta's eyes narrowed. She angrily walked toward me, but I didn't expect violence from her and was not braced for any.

(What the hell are you doing here?) she asked.

(What are you doing? The Area Guard is about to breach those doors in less than five Earth minutes) I reminded.

(Trying to get Ilic to shut down those beasts, permanently, but he got away) she fumed.

(It's not worth this, Pitta. We are guests at this place. This sets a bad precedence for Urb and all who comes after) I thought.

(I don't care about that. I figure if I destroy the beasts your dream will not come true) she thought.

I sighed and dropped my head. I looked back at where the beasts did lie and thought about her plan to stop the future.

THE MAN WHO DIDN'T WANT TO GO TO EARTH

(You are anticipating a future that hasn't happened yet. You could be causing the same future you dread, thought of that?) I asked.
She only sighed and looked upward but didn't see Nesh and Hut standing next to Lady Aisha.
(You should be watching the young ones, not down here with me) she thought.
I peered up and became instantly worried. I could not fathom where they had gone. Pitta boiled within about Ilic. I then knew she would kill him if she could find him.

(I'm close to finding him. He believes he can go silent internally, but he is very noisy in his quiet) she turned over some chairs and legs as he tried to shrink under a long table (Found him)
I heard an odd sound and turned around to see eight feet of jaws, long arms and legs. Their bodies were dark and seemed to block out the ceiling lights.
They moved almost in sync with each other. One stepped and the other stepped in unison. They didn't growl but hissed as if they were large Earth snakes.
Then, Ilic stood to be noticed with an electronic pad.
(Get them) he thought.
Pitta and I ran as two monsters tried to cut us off before getting to the door. I knew we would not make it, so I slid under a panel, lost my protective helmet as it rolled, and the monster kicked it in anger so that it bounced against the wall and spun.

THE MAN WHO DIDN'T WANT TO GO TO EARTH

Pitta vanished from sight as one creature, unbalanced by weight and inertia crashed into a nearby wall.

I used this time to emerge and run to a hidden room where Pitta stood and gestured. Will I make it? I could hear rough footsteps as I quickly slid in, and she sealed the door with her hand.

When one creature crashed into the gray door we jerked back, not sure if it would hold. Then it seemed to give up focus and lumber off.

We stood in the semi-dark as we listened for more footsteps. When Lady Aisha's face appeared above my face.

(We are breaching. Stay low) she thought.

Two doors slid open and concussion bombs slid forward to disable the beasts. Mini explosions erupted as they stood in the dimmed lights, motionless as their skin bubbled.

The Area Guard moved in, eight strong and positioned their weapons. The creatures remained suddenly motionless; their skin bubbled with energy.

"I think they are generating, or something," one guard said into his microphone.

"Take them down. Cannot take any chances," Aisha said.

The guard began to fire bursts of laser fire at the creatures, which fell under the tumult. Ilic, terrified and disorientated crawled to a far corner and peered as if in a daze.

"Creatures are down, Lady," Commander Silgan said.

THE MAN WHO DIDN'T WANT TO GO TO EARTH

Suddenly a long arm moved through the fog and grabbed a soldier and tightened arms so that the man screamed and died.

Ilic crawled backwards, not sure what was happening. His lips trembled as more men were crushed between long arms and their bodies tossed. Some were kicked and others tackled as if in a football game.

Bodies tackled fell against bulkheads, broken and bloodied they were kicked by the beasts as they gained ground. The remaining soldiers shot full laser blasts that staggered them.

When they regenerated in seconds they stomped toward their prey and crushed them as their bodies trembled in shock and pain.

With two heads they picked and chose which direction was most available until there were only two men who begged to be saved.

Until a far door opened, and Pitta stepped through with a long, dark weapon that blasted into the creatures who screeched and backed away as Lin grabbed Ilic and pulled him into the room and Pitta followed them and the door sealed.

Two men who begged to be saved ran through an open door and it was sealed as the monsters crashed it against it and hissed in anger that echoed throughout the facility.

(Now, will you tell me how to disable them?) Pita asked Ilic.

Hut and Nesh slid across a back wall and slid under a panel in the wall as Nesh touched the buttons and it opened.

(You will have to tell me how you did that) Hut thought.

THE MAN WHO DIDN'T WANT TO GO TO EARTH

(Don't have time. My mother taught me in three long turns) she thought and slid into the darkness (Need light to see)
(I'm sorry) Hut thought in his nervous tension.
He sealed the square entrance and fumbled with the tiny powerful flashlight. As they looked around her eyes widened.
(What about rats?) she asked.
His eyes widened, frightened (I don't know if they have them here. Earth rats are three times the size of our rodents on Urb and much meaner, but I don't see any rat droppings or the scurrying of feet. We should be fine, but don't quote me on that)
(I don't see any) she looked at an electronic panel (We are not far from a chute that will lead us into the middle to save our parents)
(Long as it doesn't lead us to the monsters) he thought.
(It will lead us to the monsters, that is the whole point of saving our parents from them. Are you really ready for this?) she asked.
(Ready as I can be) he thought, anguished.

Ilic tried to stand as he explained the creatures were not capable of violence.
(I don't know what happened. It must be a virus applied when it is connected to Earth circuits) he thought.
(Apparently you were wrong, now how do you kill them?) Pitta asked.
(My panel was damaged in the raid, so I will have to go online and use a backdoor) Ilic thought.
She touched a few buttons and several view screens emerged. I saw Lady Aisha as she

THE MAN WHO DIDN'T WANT TO GO TO EARTH

explained heavy artillery was about to be introduced, but I raised my hand and asked her to stand that down.

(We are trying to disable the creatures from this point. We just need a few minutes) I thought.

(We had two men survive out of eight, those are odds are unacceptable) Lady Aisha glared with angry eyes (You have five minutes)

I sighed as her face vanished and stepped from dimmed lights until my face was filled with view screen lights of blue and green images.

Ilic stared with confused eyes (What happened to my code? It's been changed, well before I took the cargo. The only one capable of changing my code was my friend, Geta. I can now see what he saw. The code was hidden in the Earth circuits not capable of being seen on our Galactic circuits)

(It looks like he placed information on the Superhuman invasion of Earth in 2153 and the Giant Feet invasion of 2171, certain characteristics they used, the crushing of individuals, the senseless violence. He must have seen you coming and anticipated it) she thought.

Ilic suddenly dropped his eyes and did not respond for a while until she screamed at him to help her!

(What's the next step?) she asked.

He closed his eyes and trembled in the violence, betrayal and deaths, he opened them and stared as if on another world, looking down.

(Termination code1987) he thought.

(How do you apply it?) she asked.

THE MAN WHO DIDN'T WANT TO GO TO EARTH

(My coder is broken. If I can get to the coder, fix it, and introduce it they will terminate) he thought as he closed his eyes, defeated.

(Where is the broken coder?) she asked as she looked around.

He pointed outward, beyond the room as we all peered past the monsters to a square object, cracked under a long desk.

(Oh no) I thought (Now you see why I didn't want to go to Earth?)

30

The young ones crawled for what seemed like forever, until Hut gave a sound of frustration through his lips.

(Do you know where you are going?) he asked.

(Do you?) she paused and looked left and right (I think it is this way)

"Breach, breach," Aisha commanded.

Extra soldiers in green and black uniforms breached each of the two doors with concussion bombs and electronic grenades. Blasts and explosions erupted until the creatures fell back with their skin on fire.

Men and women blasted them down with rapid fire to finish them off, until Aisha from her point was satisfied.

(Now *I know* where I am going) Nesh admitted as she reversed her crawl.

(Now *I know* where we are going after all that noise) Hut admitted.

She moved both hands and the panel unscrewed and suctioned into her hands like glue. Hut stared, amazed.

(Cool) Hut thought.

She placed the panel against the wall, peered in and noticed a vacuum tube that connected to the ceiling.

(Not very stable) Hut noticed.

(If we are going to save our parents, we will have to take this route) she thought.

Below them Pitta looked up as she felt the presence of her daughter.

(Nesh?) she asked.

(Mother, where are you?) Nesh asked.

(Obviously close enough to notice your thoughts) Pitta walked around the room, looking up.

Lin looked up as he noticed his son was close.

(Father?) Hut asked.

(Where are you?) Lin asked.

(About to go in a chute above the room) Hut admitted.

(Don't do that. Stay where you are. Let us find you) Lin thought.

(Tap your floor's bottom) Pitta thought.

Hut tapped it with his flashlight. Below Pitta and Lin gravitated to a corner. When Aisha arrived with several soldiers, they asked them to find their young ones.

A young female soldier stepped forward and used electronics to find them.

"They are above us by one floor in the adjoining chutes," she said.

"Get them," Aisha said.

Ilic walked carefully from the room to look down at his creation in parts of the floor. They steamed and did not move. Har entered the room with Char and cursed, but Aisha was unforgiving.

"Secure these three into the Other-Worldly Alien Interment Lockdown until they see a judge for their schemes and plans, which caused deaths and destruction in our facility," she said.

THE MAN WHO DIDN'T WANT TO GO TO EARTH

Har knew his blocking techniques would not save him from the gavel of Human justice and he didn't try to struggle.

Tall sentries that looked clear and floated, added a secure helmet on their heads to block thoughts and wrist restraints. Ilic felt fear of what was to come, while Char felt strange to not be able to flip his odd coin, as it bounced to the floor and rolled next to creature body parts.

I didn't know if things were going to get worse when it came to the news reports or the many individuals who stood about our room in awe of what we went through. It was unnerving to all of us and Lady Aisha, seeing our discomfort, elected a way out.

(It was not your fault of what was to come) she thought in our rooms through view screen (You should stay in my guess house until things die down. It would be much safer for you. Never know the minds of individuals)

We immediately agreed, thanked her profusely and began to pack to move.

Lady Aisha's house was a blue and white structure of several levels. Our temporary structure, which was the guest house was white and green with two levels and only rested several yards from her adobe.

(In a short time, through online instruction I began to learn the metric system and other ways to measure distance).

(I am proud of you, father) my son thought and hugged me deeply.

THE MAN WHO DIDN'T WANT TO GO TO EARTH

(I am here. I should learn all I can about the place) I thought, then I didn't feel so good and began to administer a needle filled with green fluid.

(Feeling better?) Hut asked, concerned.

(I do) I admitted.

(With all that has happened maybe we should cut the vacation short and return home) he thought.

(We have no home to return to) I thought (Our home was a hiding spot. It has been destroyed. An Urbanite died)

My eyes looked to my son, who stared and understood of the hidden emotions on death earlier.

(You did what you had to do for your family) Hut thought and sat next to me and bowed his head (We cannot stay here forever. We will run out of the solution in about a week. What will we do then?)

(We will have no reason but to return to our area to offset the effects of Earth's light gravity. There are other hidden mountains on Pro we can utilize. I know some friends who may hide us) I thought (For now we should try and enjoy our time here)

He made a sound of discuss between his teeth, rose and was gone within seconds. I remained sitting as Pitta sat next to me.

(My turn) she thought.

I only smiled faintly.

(You have been down on yourself about this Earth Excursion. Who knows what would have happened if you did not leave. You could be dead; we could be dead. Everything has a reason behind it) she thought.

(What a complete disaster this has been) I thought as tears fell from my white eyes and I wiped them away.

Then Lady Aisha appeared on screen with a broad smile. I could not fathom what the smile was for, but it had a deeper meaning than I could ever know.

(Meet me at my place in a few moments) she thought (Come alone, *Great Distributor*)

Pitta stared at me, and I stared at her, totally confused. I had not heard that term for a very long time.

What now? I asked as I readied myself for another blow I probably could not take.

31

I stood in a living area of servant robots, view screens and comfortable couches of blue and white designs.

Lady Aisha arrived with a tall Phasee servant in blue and white robes. He did not say anything, but I could sense he was like a mental guard as well as physical security.

(You may sit, Mr. Lin) she gestured.

I sat on the edge of the couch; sure, something was coming I could barely handle. She sat across from me with a smile I could not read, because she was advanced in hidden thoughts and emotions, probably better than Har.

(No, he taught me the ways of hidden emotions and thoughts) she replied after reading my thoughts (But he overplayed his hand. He was here over one-hundred years ago, teaching the natives, Humans mind you, how to block thoughts from Phasees and Fumans)

(He said he was here before) I admitted.

(He wanted to give the Humans an upper hand, but all it did was give some, his pupils better ways to deceive and scheme so that others did not find of their nefarious ways until it was too late) she smiled weakly (He left not on good terms and vowed to return with a better proposal that could be used like economics. That didn't work out, but enough about him. What about you?)

I felt tense. I was not sure what she was leading up to.

(What about me?) I asked.

She stood and sat closer to me with a broad smile. I felt a sense of joy and wonder as she

THE MAN WHO DIDN'T WANT TO GO TO EARTH

stared. I wanted that sense but could not find it now.

(You are the Great Distributor on Phaes, Urb, Pro and Jan. You really don't have a home to go too, due to the Fuman annihilation, something you risked your life to stop) she dropped her eyes then stared up at me (What if I give you a proposal to stay on Earth and be a distributor?)

I didn't see that coming. I stood and walked in a circle, unsure.

(What about the injections to stay healthy?) I asked (We will run out in a week)

(Our injections last one month and have less side effects. You max out the intake in two years, after that you will have to return home, like I did before Phaes was destroyed. After six months I returned to Earth and started all over again) she admitted.

I was not so sure, and she surprised me with more information about Pitta's hostage situation.

(You know she could be charged with hostage taking. That is an automatic five-year sentence. I will rescind that order if you take my offer up) she thought.

I returned to the guest house, twisted within on what to do, but in the end I took it up, especially for the sake of Pitta.

(Thank you) she said and gave me a deep hug.

(It's a good deal) Hut thought.

I took the deal, and wondered if there were hidden motives, I didn't see.

Of course, I was right.

Again.

THE MAN WHO DIDN'T WANT TO GO TO EARTH

Other-Worldly Alien Interment Lockdown or OWAIL was a system of temporary jails designed in 2102 by Aisha and Bokade Lute for interworld travel of derelict Other-Worldly beings.

There were in 2186 over ten OWAIL'S worldwide, able to intercept Other Worldly Aliens, examine their intentions and incarcerate the bad ones, then send them back through the wormhole and release the good ones into society to hopefully improve on Human conditions.

Laws designed were connected to internment camps on the former Phaes, and its cousin planets: Jan, Pro, and Urb.

Many Humans, shaken to their core by the spider-crab wars were fearful and allowed Aisha and Bokade, free reign in keeping derelict Other-Worldly aliens at bay.

Bokade Lute from the decedent line of the Bolaris was a distant cousin of Luther Reams and gained much respect when he stopped the slaughter of the Bolaris after they left the battlefield in their defeat from rough man Mars (then called Maurice).

He was a tall Bolaris (almost seven feet) with hairy features and a muscular frame. He rarely expressed his thoughts through words but gestures of the face and body movements.

So, when Bokade and Aisha visited Ilic's cell he stood from a long bed and brushed down his dingy robes with dirty hands.

(Sorry for the grime) Ilic thought.

"You have the means to speak through the mouth, English? You have studied and complied with the requirements of Earth travel; I presume?" Aisha asked, though she knew the answer.

Ilic appeared nervous and moved his mouth slowly but sounds barely came out.

"Try again," Aisha said firmly.

Bokade sighed, stared, and waited.

(I don't know) Ilic resumed in thoughts.

"Try again," Aisha pressed.

Ilic sighed and moved his mouth and more clearer words traveled.

"Again," she said.

"I'm trying...," he said, barely.

"Much better," she said. "Your council will be Bokade Lute, here. He has over eighty years in handling derelict aliens from other worlds. You will meet a judge in one month to state your case.

"Found guilty you can be given up to two years interment and extradition to your planet of choice or you can be given death if the crime is found to be heinous, such as six dead Humans are. Do you understand the gravity of your crimes?" she asked.

"I do," he forced.

"Another language besides English to learn on Earth is Spanish and a third is Chinese. You can learn them in only a few moments with our systems and Urb memory recall," she turned to leave with Bokade, but Ilic raised his hand, and she turned back.

"I-I didn't know they were going to be violent," he said. "I didn't design them to do that."

"I know," she said with a softer voice, her eyes became gentle. "Use the facilities to stay clean. It reflects on us whether you are healthy or not."

THE MAN WHO DIDN'T WANT TO GO TO EARTH

When they left, he looked around the jail cell and saw clear and white areas and a bathroom of light reflected from the walls. He was pleased he was alone and took folded blue garbs from the cot and began to wash and cry, alone.

Har did use the facilities to wash and to change into blue garbs of short sleeves and long pants. His damaged robes of sweat and cuts made as robots stepped on their hems, was tossed in a chute that disappeared underground.

(Nice accommodations for a planet on the edge of destruction) he thought.

He heard a slight hum and ignored it and stared at himself in the mirror.

"You think we are near destruction, old friend?" Aisha asked from behind him.

When he turned around, he saw Aisha and Bokade as they stood in green and black robes. He assumed they used the electronic bars to move in and out of cells.

He could tell immediately Bokade was Bolaris and connected to Luther Beams.

Skilled in several languages from his last sojourn, Har found no problem in moving his lips and pushing sounds he did not make for nearly 100 years.

"Yes, I think the Earth is way overdue for destruction," Har thought. "That is why I came with the ultimate in defense, before it blew up in my face."

"Ah, but there were repercussions in what you did. It could be death from a deal gone awry.

THE MAN WHO DIDN'T WANT TO GO TO EARTH

Six men died, Human at that. I must make an example of someone.

"Since Ilic was the pawn in this game guess who will be picked to take the fire of death and who will be sent off planet?" she asked slyly.

"I know I may be the scapegoat in the quest for Human justice. I do not have a good track record when it comes to Human endeavors, despite the fact I helped them to block themselves from our kind for nearly a century. What compensation do I get for that?" he asked.

"You were paid handsomely for your teachings I am sure," she said.

"It was not enough," he growled.

"You have one month before you see the judge. Bokade will be your council. Use him to your betterment," she said.

Char changed out of his clothes, washed and combed his black hair back, when he heard the bars' part, they made an odd sound that startled him, almost like a humming...

He walked from the bathroom to greet Aisha and Bokade. They all stood silently for a moment, no thoughts or lip movements, until...

"Hello," Char said. "I believe you want to communicate in English. I know Chinese, Spanish and Korean. Bokade will be my council?"

Bokade nodded and half-bowed in acknowledgement.

"I see you have been studying our protocols," she said.

"Easy to learn, but I found Korean to be a bit *challenging*," Char said.

THE MAN WHO DIDN'T WANT TO GO TO EARTH

There was a deeper silence as Char gathered his thoughts as they moved to his lips.

"I have a request," he said.

"You want your flip coin," she said. "You use it to make decisions that are hard to make."

"It helps me," he said in clipped tones.

"There should be no problem in gaining your coin," she said. "You have one month before you see the judge, maybe the coin can help you with what words to say."

"It's only for yes and no answers, nothing as complex as that," Char admitted.

She only nodded and left with Bokade as Char slightly smiled, pleased he will gain his flip coin again.

THE MAN WHO DIDN'T WANT TO GO TO EARTH

32

I was floored as I studied all the responsibilities I would gain while Regional Director of Guatemala.

I studied blue and green screens because they were supposed to be better on the eyes, but my eyes became filled with blood by midnight and I had to shut down the system to rest.

I sat in semi-darkness and thought of nothing, until I noticed a dark figure to my left. I immediately became alarmed, but Pitta stepped forward and by a dim overhead light she smiled.

(You are set to kill me by heart failure) I thought.

She sat next to me and patted my leg affectionately.

(You are too tightly wound. Everything came out well, so far) she admitted.

(So far) I nodded (As Regional Director I would oversee this entire area, then it is supposed to increase every ten years, but I won't be here in ten years, sticking to the two years. When I go back, I go back *for good*)

She understood and sat quietly for a time.

(I sometimes think this was all planned somehow) she thought.

I stared at her with confused eyes.

(What are you talking about?) I asked (No one could have planned this debacle. It has been a disaster from beginning to end)

(Has it?) she asked.

I sat, intrigued.

(Look, it seemed to start when your son asked to go to Earth, but what if it started before that? Did you not have to meet the Council of Elders six medium turns ago about going to Earth to become a great distributor and you refused?) she asked.

(Yes, turned them down) I thought, proud of my firmness.

(I have no proof, but it all seems so pat. They ask for your help. You refuse. You end up on Earth doing the exact thing they asked of you. There are no coincidences in life) she thought.

I shook my head negatively.

(I don't buy it) I thought.

(Of course, it didn't come out quite as they planned, but whatever does?) she asked.

I stared at her with insane eyes of confusion and disbelief. I smiled and waved her thoughts away, but inside I seethed with questions.

I wanted to visit Lady Aisha before the day resumed in its full fury. I did not sleep much and when I entered her adobe my exhaustion showed on my face.

Aisha looked like her beautiful self of long, golden hair, skin that was tanned and the prominent white eyes and large forehead of all Phasees.

She stood in gold and blue robes that fell to her small feet. When she walked it appeared like she was gliding, but I attributed that to her graceful movements and quiet demeanor.

"You may need to sit down for a moment, or you look like you are going to fall down," she said.

I had to adjust my mouth to speak, because I assumed she wanted to speak English.

THE MAN WHO DIDN'T WANT TO GO TO EARTH

"The more you practice the better you will become. You are concerned about some raised issues when it comes to the Elders on Urb. Yes, they did some manipulation. They knew of your son's desire to study Earth History and to possibly go there," she sat, and I sat, shocked.

"So, they manipulated my son?" I asked, enraged.

"No, they didn't do such a thing. Your mother is on the Council. She knew of your son's desire to go to Earth. They notified a classmate to talk about going to Earth, which is Nesh, then it went from there," she said.

"That's manipulation of a young one," I said, angry, betrayed.

"Call it what you want. It got you here, didn't it?" she admitted.

"A place I didn't really want to be and almost dead-on top of it," I said angrier.

I fumed silently for a moment as I played each scenario in my head. She gave me ample time to digest it all and did not interfere.

"So, this is about Earth Domination?" I asked much calmer.

"Not domination, but a better world through Urb manipulation. They are thinking long term. A better Earth is best for the entire region and can affect Urb much later," she said.

"A better Earth can stave off an Earthling invasion of Urb," I thought.

"Something like that," she said.

I sat for some time as my thoughts went in a whirlwind. She peered at me, apparently reading my thoughts and sensing my emotions.

THE MAN WHO DIDN'T WANT TO GO TO EARTH

"You may revise that two-year deal and stay the ten for a better fit. It only takes a swing back and forth between planets every two years, and a six-month acclimation back into Earth vibes," she admitted.

I felt betrayed and wanted no parts of extra time. I rose and only nodded before I left to simmer in my anger.

"He is not settled yet, but he is getting there," Aisha said on the view screen.

She observed ten Elder Council members who sat in green and black robes in a semi-circle on stone steps.

"I know you like your Earth languages, and the best is English, so we will communicate as you wish," Nodal, (834) the lead council member said with barely a movement of his lips, a dark tall frame and white eyes.

"I am looking forward to your visit here in five long turns, which should make it about four years, here. You should be well-prepared in all the major languages," she said.

"It almost didn't happen," Tonna, a female council member and Lin's mother said. "What was Har and his crew thinking of?"

"It was about the money with them." she said, then looked at a weakening signal. "We will lose reception in a few minutes. The communication probe is dying. Any last words?"

"Sounds so final," Nodal said.

"It could be final for us if Earth finds a way to use the wormhole without Other-Worldly Alien technology, which according to their scientists is only a few years away. With their hostile genes and history, we would not last that long in a firefight," she thought.

"We always have a preemptive strike in our pocket. Hit them while they are still vulnerable," Tonna said firmly.

"Not while the blues are still in control. There are over 892 blues on Earth, and if they knew we were going to strike first, they would withhold technology that could cripple our system, no, this is the best play," Aisha said.

"Harmonic Aliens love them some Humans, don't they?" Tonna asked.

"It's their new project. There was a time not too long ago when we were like Humans; hostile, and ready to go war in an instant," Nodal said.

"What will become of my friend Har?" Tonna asked. "I have known him for over one-hundred and thirty-one long turns."

The other Council members, including Nodal, had known him for just as long.

Aisha's eyes glazed over with sadness and a determination that was difficult to read over light years.

"He is near playing his last hand. There isn't much hope for him and his crew," Aisha allowed the blue probe to disintegrate as it met certain atmospheric pressures, which it was designed to do, and it left no trace of its existence.

This dissolved their image both ways as the Council sat in silence and disbelief, they could do nothing for their colleague and friend.

THE MAN WHO DIDN'T WANT TO GO TO EARTH

<u>33</u>

Har stood quietly in his jail cell of bright lights that illuminated the floor and walls. He could not imagine a time when jail cells had barely any features like running water or a toilet and rats and roaches. He shuddered to think of a time like that on Earth, maybe over 400 years ago.

He wondered about his connection to Char who was supposed to connect through his coin, so they could bargain their way out. He wondered what took him so long.

He knew Aisha and the others did not know how valuable the coin was or they would not have retrieved it for their friend. He knew this by senses only, not mind connections, which made matters worse.

To Har senses were full of assumptions and he did not like to go by assumptions, too many variables.

(I don't like to assume, old friend) Har thought (Let's play this game so we can go home)

Char stared at the thick object and sighed within. He was not sure if he wanted to do it. He knew if he went through with the action, and it didn't work they could be stuck on Earth until they were forced to rotate back in two years.

(Here goes nothing) Char stood and flipped the object in his rough hands, then he laid it on the bars and the bars parted with a slight hum (Nice touch)

He extracted the coin and flipped it as he walked carefully four cell doors down.

THE MAN WHO DIDN'T WANT TO GO TO EARTH

(Old friend) Char stood before electronic bars but did not see Har until he placed the coin on its bars, so that it separated and showed Har standing within.

(What took you so long?) Har asked, as he stepped forward.

(A thank you is in order) Char inquired, chagrined.

(After we escaped. Let's not get ahead of ourselves) Har thought as he refused to thank him.

(The system has a delay of five tiny turns that the flip has compensated for. We have that long to find a ship and get the hell off planet) Char thought.

(I already have our ship in mind. It's where they are keeping our hidden cargo. I saw it through mental schematics of Aisha's mind) Har thought.

(She could be misleading us) Char thought.

(It's all we have) Har thought (Follow me)

(We are forgetting someone) Char thought of Ilic.

(We have no time to get him. We don't need him anymore. When we get the cargo I have the codes, that's all we will need; now let's go before we run out of time) Har thought.

They walked for what seemed like forever, while Char read his flip coin that gave off schematics and timed performance in the system.

(One tiny turn left) Char thought as his anxiety rose.

(Here already) Har stood before a dark gray door and pressed his hand against illuminated buttons as the door hissed apart.

(You must show me how you do that) Char stared, impressed.

THE MAN WHO DIDN'T WANT TO GO TO EARTH

(Only for my most ardent students) Har and Char walked in just as the system came online to show real time.

(We are officially gone from their screens. We had better move fast) Char thought.

Har stared about, not sure which direction to go, because the ship was small, and it had many twists and turns. He expected to see the cargo once they entered the vessel and when he did not, he "assumed" it was nearby in another room.

He quickly moved to a curved green panel and moved his hands over the panel so that the ship powered up and its engines revved.

Char smiled broadly and turned in a circle, but he didn't notice the cargo. Har was trying to move the ship from its dock into space, but its locking clamps did not reverse.

(What the hell?) Har asked.

(Why isn't it moving?) Char asked.

(Because you *assumed*) a thought entered their minds simultaneously.

Har and Char turned in a circle, not sure where the thought emanated from. Then, when an overhead view screen came on Aisha frowned with Arn2, both looked disappointed.

(Why would you *assume* I would leave open my mind for you to pick? You taught me better than that) she thought (Did you not find me an apt pupil?)

(I should have known. It was too easy) Har thought.

Char threw his hands in the air and sighed.

(Do we go back to jail?) Char asked, defeated.

THE MAN WHO DIDN'T WANT TO GO TO EARTH

(No) Aisha said solemnly (You escaped, remember?)
(I don't understand) Char admitted.

Har closed his eyes, then sat down and accepted what was to become of them. Char glared at him, not understanding.

(She is letting us go. You need to operate the controls) Char thought.

Aisha touched a button, and the docking clamps were released so that the ship hovered and began to spin. Char moved his hand over the panel and tried to gain control, but to no avail.

(I really need some help here, friend. Controls are offline and I cannot gain traction. Get your ass out of that seat and give me a hand, will you?) Char asked.

Har stared at him with hard eyes of disbelief.

(She removed the control settings you idiot. We have no control) Har thought.

Char looked from screen to screen and knew the end was near as the ship began to fill with internal and external pressures. He then sat next to his friend and flipped his thick coin.

(Guess I don't need this anymore) Char was about to toss it behind him (No, I'll keep it just in case I need it on the other side of life)

Har glared at him and thought and said nothing as the ship tossed violently above the atmosphere and erupted debris that floated in bits to the ocean below.

(Goodbye, old friend) Aisha thought with sadness and blanked the screen.

THE MAN WHO DIDN'T WANT TO GO TO EARTH

Ilic was surprised when he heard a slight hum as he laid in dimmed lights. When he rose to greet any visitors, he saw it was Aisha, Arn2 and Bokade. They withheld any thoughts he could use, and stared blankly, which left him in the dark.

"I am not reading anything from you three. You are either ghosts or images in my head, which one is it?" Ilic asked.

"We are neither. We are here to inform you your friends are dead. Prison break didn't go so well. You are the last of them all. For some reason they didn't include you in the break. Would you have participated? I wonder...," she paused in her words.

Ilic sighed deeply and shook his head from side to side, stunned and saddened.

"They didn't include me because I would not have gone with them. Better to take my whipping and get it out of the way like my mother used to say, God Bless her soul, she died in the Phaes Destruction," Ilic said.

"I am sorry for your loss," Aisha touched his arm tenderly. "You said something about taking your whipping. Were you whipped as a child, Mr. Ilic?"

Ilic's eyes brightened as he thought of a distant past.

"No, I was never whipped, but I was taught to pay for my mistakes starting at eleven long turns," he said.

Aisha became intrigued by his words and walked closer as she peered into his face.

"I can see a lot of things did not go well in your life, most from bad decisions not of your making. I can see you stole the cargo from your

THE MAN WHO DIDN'T WANT TO GO TO EARTH

friend because he wanted to make the creatures violent and included a virus that resembled the Superhumans on Earth and the Giant Feet debacle of 2171.

"They were violent not of your making and without your knowledge. That goes to your favor," she said.

"That is right," he replied, not sure if he wanted to say more.

"I am willing to work with your prison sentence if you can do me one favor," she said.

"Anything," he said, encouraged.

THE MAN WHO DIDN'T WANT TO GO TO EARTH

34

I am the man who didn't want to go to Earth; but I am trying to make the best of it as I went along with trips with my son; Hut, Pitta's daughter, Nesh and Pitta. We tried to gel as a family as much as possible.

When I heard of the deaths of Char and Har, Pitta's teacher, I was greatly saddened. It appeared on the internet as an accident; but with the connections to the monster debacle Pitta and I did not believe it was an accident.

(They tried to escape with the cargo, that is the story pushed) Pitta thought, anguished (Aisha is a lot more cunning and deadly than I presumed she was)

(She is connected to the rough man, and they are no joke when it comes to winning) I turned to her (You should know)

She was calmly sitting next to me and stood, angered and betrayed by my words. I suspected a beat down at any moment; but she withheld her blows and left the room in a huff.

I sat for some time in sunlight and view screen images until I hoped she was calm enough to receive me. I rose and walked into a far room of one long bench and a balcony.

She sat with her back to me, and I carefully made my way next to her and touched her hand.

(I am sorry. That was insensitive of me) I thought.

(No) she rubbed my hand (I should not be so sensitive when it comes to Mars, after all he is the father of my only child)

THE MAN WHO DIDN'T WANT TO GO TO EARTH

(Does she know about her father?) I asked, carefully.

(Only that he is dead) she admitted (I could not tell her more, too graphic. He led a violent life to keep all of us safe. Maybe when she is older)

I remained silent and watched as air vehicles floated above Lady Aisha's blue and white structure and some landed to produce individuals in colorful robes.

(Looks like an entourage) I thought as I peered closer from the second ledge (Can't tell from here, but looks like some important individuals)

She suddenly stood as if she saw a ghost, I stared upward, not sure how to respond.

(Is everything okay?) I asked.

(That's him) she thought and leaped from the second ledge as her robes flapped onto the grass below.

I stood for some time and did not follow her, immediately, but took an elevator down.

She reached the entourage, but not before the protective robots moved forward and gave warning. She raised her hands in submission, as I expected laser fire to come her way any moment.

Pitta stared with her mouth open, stunned as three figures moved toward her, despite the robot's warning and coming too close. A dark, short figure raised his hand and the robots extracted backward with hand weapons lowered...

He smiled with broad teeth and gentle white eyes. His hair was combed back and white. With Phasee features his forehead projected sweat in

THE MAN WHO DIDN'T WANT TO GO TO EARTH

the warmth of this day. His robes were green and blue with dark flexies that covered his feet.

It was Mars!

(You died) she thought.

"I did die. I am his clone," Mars said.

(What? I thought that is illegal on Urb and the other planets) she thought.

"Not on planet Earth, free will zone, not governed by the Universal Planet Operation Laws," Ntb said.

"We try to use vocals on Earth as much as possible, preferably English in this region," Mars said.

"Technically, it's Spanish in this region," Arn2 admitted. "We are in Guatemala."

"Oh," Mars shrugged his shoulders. "You are right. We can all talk Spanish if you want."

Ntb, the former companion of Mars introduced his clone with a touch on the shoulder and shrugged off speaking other than English for now.

"Hi, Pitta, he did die on the way to Earth, but we had extracted DNA for a possible clone on Earth. We were banned for doing so on Urb and the other planets due to faults in the science, but Earth's a free will zone," Ntb said.

"Ntb, and Mars2 this is Pitta's companion, Lin and now their son and daughter…," Arn2 trailed in his words.

"We are not companions," Lin said uncomfortably.

Pitta shrugged off Lin's words of denying their companionship and carefully turned about as Nesh, and Hut walked up. Hut looked excited and

THE MAN WHO DIDN'T WANT TO GO TO EARTH

Nesh appeared horrified that her father who was dead was now alive.

"You are supposed to be dead," Hut said.

"I get that a lot," Mars2 said.

"He's a clone," Lin admitted in low tones to his son.

"Wow," Hut walked almost under Mars2. "Do you retain all of his memories?"

"Most of them. I do not retain his soul. I am just a carbon copy of him, almost like an echo of what he was," Mars2 said.

There was a deep silence as they all stood and reflected on this, until Nesh approached him and carefully hugged him about the waist until he hugged her back.

Pitta covered her mouth to try and contain her grief as tears welled and fell. This startled Lin who was not used to seeing the tough Pitta cry so openly. He then surmised she really loved Mars, deeply.

Ilic was not sure what Lady Aisha had in mind when she asked for a favor because she was not specific and with the ability to hide emotions and thoughts, she could be evasive as ever and he would not know the difference.

It was near a month since the monster incident and his friends died. His court day was only in a few days, and he would have to state his case; but Aisha arrived with Bokade and Arn2 and they all appeared to be happy.

This he could not fathom from the former tragedies and when they gathered in a long, well-lit room with high ceilings and two long containers on the floor. He then knew why they smiled.

THE MAN WHO DIDN'T WANT TO GO TO EARTH

"The cargo," Ilic peered down.

It laid in bits and pieces and appeared as a jumble of arms and legs, only the heads were connected by broken shoulders and did not disassemble.

"You are in charge of reassembling them with the Superhuman and Giant Feet virus removed and making them work like they should, without violence," Aisha emphasized.

"We will commute your sentence until further notice," Arn2 said.

"That way those six individuals who died did not die in vain," Bokade said.

"Can you do it?" she asked.

Ilic nodded and said he could. Arn2 patted him on the back.

"I will give you as much help as I can. They are fascinating creatures," Arn2 said.

"Thank you, Arn," Ilic patted his shoulder.

"No, I am Arn2, now. I was informed I must use the two to signify a clone. It was adjusted in my matrix," Arn2 said.

"Okay," Ilic said. "Arn2 it is."

"Now, this is your time to shine, Mr. Ilic, what will you do with it?" Aisha asked, even though she knew.

"I will do the best that I can," Ilic said.

"Good answer," Aisha said and turned to the others for confirmation.

THE MAN WHO DIDN'T WANT TO GO TO EARTH

<u>35</u>

<u>Planet Urb</u>

Tonie wanted all things to settle in the region as when it came to her father's death and the placing in power of her two brothers, Faro and Tepa, who acted in a dual role.

She had one more card to play and moved very carefully to present it less they figure her plan and block it.

She arrived with Tepa's two communicators, Shoad and Arap, who walked in blue and white robes and green boots.

The ten Elders sat in various groups from younger to older, so that two groups remained. The younger group of Tonna and three other members communicated in one corner as Nodal and the older members connected in another.

Faro was signing an order mentally on the view screen while Tepa appeared bored, but when he saw his two communicators his eyes lit up with alarm.

(Why are they here?) he asked as he stood.

(They are here, because of you, brother) Tonie thought (They kept records of your pursuits in female persuasions. You assaulted them against Urb Law, but used the protection of father to stay alive)

She adjusted a signal, and several images came on the view screen of him trying to force himself on Shoad and Arap at different times when they were alone.

With some quick thinking and maneuvering they removed themselves from the situation, but there were instances when females could not and were raped.

(What the hell are you talking about?) Tepa asked (I am now leader of the high council. Any charges are scrapped once I am in office)

(No, these charges were placed before you became leader, so they are valid. Charges during the leadership can be rescinded) Tonie thought.

The Elders looked with interest but did not interfere, curious, they wondered how this scenario would play out.

Tepa turned to the council, but they made no moves to stop events, fearful he turned to Faro, who rose to protest, but Tonie raised her hand.

(If you protest, brother I have records of you doing small deeds for father that could place you in a bad light. It would be best if you say nothing at this time) Tonie thought and waved robots toward Tepa's direction.

(No, no, no) Tepa tried to run but Tonie shot him with a stun weapon so that he fell face forward and broke his long nose. As his blood oozed, she stared, horrified (I hate violence)

(You know if these charges are pushed through, he will be killed by Urb Law) Faro thought, anguished for his brother.

(I know, but the law is the law, and he has been doing this long enough. He even tried his way with me, but I rebuffed him with a knee to the genitals) she thought solemnly.

Faro sat, surprised and horrified that Tepa tried sex with his own sister.

(It happened when I was five long turns, enough to know what he did was wrong, but I could

THE MAN WHO DIDN'T WANT TO GO TO EARTH

not bring myself to tell father, it would have placed him in a bad spot, to kill his son, or send him off, never to be seen again) she sighed deeply and touched the empty chair.

Faro stared at her with new eyes and a deep sympathy for her plight.

(I kept it deep down, not to be seen in even the strongest mental priers, even father did not notice it; but it ate at me for a long time, and with the complaints from other females of rapes and other sexual assaults I planned the proper time to play my cards) she thought.

Faro sighed deeply and eyed her with deep concern. She sat in a long, gray chair and sighed (I could get used to this)

The communicators, Shoad and Arap stood behind her as instant advisors. Faro understood his power would be shared, not authoritarian as before and he sat, uneasy, but wary as the Elders stared, pleased she took charge.

Planet Earth

I was worried about taking on any new injections. I had long ago run out of my chemical concoction and knew it was a matter of time before I became deathly ill.

My son, Nesh and Pitta received their injections with only slight nausea and some dizziness, but no prophetic dreams.

I was more concerned about prophetic dreams than physical illness. As I went under, I was hoping not to see the two-headed creatures, but I did, but they were like puppy dogs and ran around as if playful.

THE MAN WHO DIDN'T WANT TO GO TO EARTH

I awakened, terrified, still and was given a green and blue substance to drink that took away any dizziness and nausea. Lady Aisha stood over me and gave me a strange stare.

"You saw something, something to do with the monsters," she said.

I only nodded, terrified, and began to look around as if they would barrel through any door to crush and afterward play as puppy dogs.

"Follow me," she gestured with her head.

"I don't want to follow you. This could be a bad dream and I don't want to be led to a slaughter," I said.

"You are not sleeping. I assure you," she said.

"They say that in all bad dreams," I replied.

"So, are you going to sit in this tube until you rot or are you going to test the waters of whether you are woken, or sleep?" she asked.

I sat for a long time and decided to follow her into a small room, where I carefully sat down, and she adjusted the screens with a wave of her hand.

"That's so cool the way you do that," I said.

"Takes years of practice. It took me almost ten years to do it right without frying all the circuits. Practice can be very expensive," she said.

"What am I looking at here?" I asked.

An electronic image moved forward, and I became entranced by colorful images and light jazz music. I expected a concert, but Ilic's image, wrapped in yellow robes and combed back brown hair, moved forward, and his mouth moved, but I couldn't hear a word he said.

"He talks so low," she moved her hand so that his words became audible.

"...I stand before you as a witness and builder of the impossible to possible. I present a new way of defending your home, office or loved ones. I present *Puppy101*," he stepped back...

I almost came out the chair, but Lady Aisha settled me down with a pat from her hand.

"Easy," she said.

Two monsters stepped forward and hissed more than a growl and turned in a circle as they seemed to advance on Ilic. I knew he was a goner as they nudged him about and he rubbed their heads and motioned for them to sit, stand and turn in a circle.

"Puppy1 and Puppy2, take me into the cage," he suddenly said.

The creatures instantly stepped back, hissed and I suspected that would be in the end of Ilic as they tore into his flesh, but this is not what happened.

Who I suspect was Puppy1 turned Ilic around and placed hidden cuffs on his arms as Puppy2 hissed and gestured to an open cage.

Ilic pretended to resist as they pushed and shoved him to an open cage, closed the cage and appeared to bark, mixed with a hiss.

"You can let me go Puppy1 and Puppy2," Ilic said.

Their countenances changed and a sneer showed teeth and their eyes lit up as they removed the cage lock and unlocked his handcuffs. He found this to be exhilarating as he turned in a circle, pleased the performance went as planned.

"Puppy101 is only on special order. You get your very own Puppy101 for thirty days free, then

THE MAN WHO DIDN'T WANT TO GO TO EARTH

you can be charged. See, they are playful as puppies," he wrestled with them in an open space of grass and trees as relaxing background music played.

When the commercial faded to black, I sat in my own thoughts for some time as Lady Aisha sat next to me in a clear chair that emitted light and placed a hand on my arm.

"You saw something similar. You are given a glimpse into a possible future, but it's not written in stone. It can change as it goes it along," she admitted.

"Yes," I agreed with a nod of my head, still unsure of what I just saw.

"You have a gift of prophecy, usually edged by certain chemicals. Without the chemicals would you still see the same? I doubt it," she said.

"The chemicals must be altering my perception of past, present, and future," I stared at her with hard eyes. "But the others saw the same future on our way here."

"Those were a combination of different chemicals, much harsher than our concoction. Their side effects last a lot longer than what we have, but you still saw something with our combination, while they did not. You are gifted," she said.

I sighed deeply and looked at my hands.

"Doesn't feel like a gift," I said.

"Let me take notes as you come out of chemical sleep for now on. I can compare what you dreamed to reality. It should be illuminating for us both," she said.

"I don't mind," I said.

"Okay," she rose from the clear chair. "Time to get you back to your companion. She may worry."

"She's not my companion. We have never gone that far, and it has not been eight long turns. According to Urb Law eight long turns is required to solidify a companionship," I said.

"Oh, she is your companion. She cares about you and 'crashed the party', so to say," she smiled, and it made her white eyes light up.

I had never seen her so happy; it unbalanced my solemn mood, and she rubbed my shoulder.

"Here on Earth are a hodgepodge of laws from different solar systems. We have marriage and companionship, night visits, you name it; but the highest on Earth is marriage. The ceremony does something to your soul," she said.

I understood and nodded, but she moved closer. I could feel the heat as it emanated from her body.

"You are a quiet, shy one, but I wouldn't mind you as a night person," she smiled, and I became instantly uneasy and stepped back.

"I don't know if I can do that," I said, alarmed.

"You have a desire for me I can tell, and I have a desire for you. That's all a night person is. It's not a commitment to each other, just a night of unending pleasure," she said.

I was at a loss for words. She rubbed my shoulder and we walked from the room, just when Pitta arrived with Nesh and Hut. Lady Aisha smiled and left as if a ghost as I stared, mortified.

THE MAN WHO DIDN'T WANT TO GO TO EARTH

I sat off to myself in my own thoughts as view screens moved about with news of the day. I had them rotate according to the breaking news and was surprised to see Ilic's commercial rotate in.

(Not that idiot) Pitta came behind me, angry to see his image (I should have killed him when I had the chance)

I was horrified by her words, and she felt my horror and sat next to me, ashamed.

(What is wrong with me when it comes to him?) she asked (I see his image and want to smash his face in)

I contemplated her words and carefully came up with a hypothesis and knew she could respond in a certain way by smashing my face in instead of Ilic's.

(You see him as the past you wanted to leave behind. It's a bloody, violent past. I don't blame you, but crushing Ilic will not crush your past, only cause it to grow bigger, soon it will only consume you) I thought (Almost like my fear of coming to Earth, it consumed me so that it became a reality)

She only nodded and I breathed a sigh of relief that my face was not used as a punching bag. When she gave me a slight hug she moved back as if repulsed. I suspected my earlier shower and teeth brush did not hold, but she made clear I did not stink.

(I see that Lady Aisha asked you to be a night person. You turned her down. You should take her up on it. It's obvious you desire her too) she thought.

(No) I thought (It seems wrong)

THE MAN WHO DIDN'T WANT TO GO TO EARTH

(Why? We are not married, and we are not companions. You constantly said so yourself) she said.

I still found the idea to be strange and rebuffed it, but deep down I wanted to go through with the action.

EPILOGUE

I somehow survived a stint of two years on Earth without further incidents of violence or war and in 2188 near 2189, before I became deathly ill; moved through the wormhole with Pitta, her daughter, Nesh and my son Hut.

We coasted at Phaes' former destruction and stared through windows as parts of it turned as if still in orbit, but each long turn it began to dissolve until only a shadow of itself remained.

Its moons destroyed acted as debris that moved in a circle so that it resembled a hodgepodge of parts and stones sifted through broken, energy.

(Scientists expect it to be gone in ten long turns) I thought to Hut who stared, fascinated.

(They gave up a lot for us in fighting the destroyers) Hut thought as his eyes became moist with sadness.

(Yes, they did. It was not in vain. We will make them proud of us by not moving towards another war) I thought.

Hut stared at me with intense eyes. He was reading my countenance well.

(Father, you want to come back to Earth for another sojourn) he became excited and hugged me partially.

(After you finish with your studies in Jan) I thought.

He pouted (Not fair)

(The same with you, Nesh) Pitta stepped from behind me and rubbed my shoulder (Your studies, first)

THE MAN WHO DIDN'T WANT TO GO TO EARTH

Nesh bowed her head and looked at the floor, disappointed.

I smiled at Pitta and kissed her on the mouth, happy we were in a companionship, finally. Missed by a few tiny turns I agreed to the arrangement and hoped for the best. If it failed, I could blame it on the lack of final turns by Urb Law.
(Can war be staved off?) Pitta asked, concerned.
I sighed deeply and thought of the past events and had hope.
(Yes) I thought with a new hope (If not we will be the first to feel it and probably not survive, being on the front line of it all)
(Then be a Great Distributor as I know you are. If not for Urb, do it for us) she thought, concerned.
(I will do my best) I thought as I had intentions of going to Earth with a new fire in my bones to stave off war.

I ONCE HAD A DREAM

I once had a dream of a creature with two heads. This was some time ago, but it stuck with me, so I included it in the book.

I was walking through an area of a variety of people, almost a hub like *Deep Space 9* (*Star Trek Plug*), when I noticed two tall creatures with dark bodies that walked through with two heads that pointed in opposite directions, long arms, long legs and a smile that appeared sinister to me.

In this dream we all seemed nonchalant and tried to relax, so that the creatures would not feel our fear or anxiety, peg us as hiding something and tear into us.

Near the end of this dream, I was always shadowed by a teacher, but this teacher stepped out and I began to feel anxiety.

A friend, displayed on a long chair, tried to teach me how to act by reading and motioning me to sit down, when the creatures walked in.

I was not guilty of anything, but anxiety and fear and I began to panic and tried to make it to the door. Of course, I was too slow and awakened in a start.

This dream taught me to take it easy in certain situations or I could make matters worse, but the dream made an impression so that I placed some parts of them in the book.

In conclusion all my books have an underlying story not explained on the surface. I do believe all stories are built the same, so this was nothing new.

THE MAN WHO DIDN'T WANT TO GO TO EARTH

In my books I tried to explain the technology of the future and how it could be used. I believe we as Humans have the potential to do as written in my books, but I pray we use this tech to better Human society instead of tearing it down.

In my books many of my characters placed themselves in hard situations and they were met with tragedy while others found themselves in bad situations without putting themselves in those situations, just like life.

Do I believe the future will be as I wrote it?

I pray not, because many individuals did not survive due to cataclysmic events and a new world developed not to our liking.

Some events may transpire as I wrote them, especially the futuristic technological part; but most will not because it is fiction with elements of science included.

What is the purpose of adding the mystery writer, when the reader already knows I am the mystery writer?

In this story the writer is encouraged to write the story of his sojourn to Earth and as an encouragement he is told he would be collaborating with a mystery writer. It could only be used as a pointer to help him do the story.

Also, characters, like real people, like to know who they are collaborating with. It gives them a point of reference, but I had no intention of appearing to the character as I did in Blue Battles and Cory's Fears.

THE MAN WHO DIDN'T WANT TO GO TO EARTH

That was weird enough but a true possibility through mind connections which has no time limits.

Every writer writes from a core within that reflects out to all the characters, almost like a bubble of energy. When the story is told the bubble becomes weak and collapses inward so that another bubble is formed for a new story.

This is the same with life. Each life we walk in a bubble of energy and when death occurs the bubble collapses and the story is finished.

I trust this answered some of your questions about my stories.

Please pass the stories along because a friend who was able to "see" said it would take a thousand years before I would see results.

Of course, he "saw" wrong. I would not be here in a thousand years. Maybe he meant ten years.

Mystery Writer 1/22/2023

THE MAN WHO DIDN'T WANT TO GO TO EARTH

<u>OTHER BOOKS BY MICHAEL LIGHTEN</u>
- The Battles of Lance the Writer
- Hateland
- Cory's Fears
- Rough Storm 2045
- Rough Man Daughters
- The Death and Life of Tobias Stone
- Care Teachings Revised (Poetry)
- Quotes & Thoughts on the 9 Attributes (Positive Ideas)
- Love Notes Battle
- Rough Wars
- Superhumans 2153
- Rough Men International 2166
- Blue Battles
- Giant Feet
- Rough Men Battles
- Mars vs Mars
- Phaes 2: The Final End